Conflict in Contention

Thomas 'DOC' Savage

Published by J.C. Hulsey Books, 2024.

This is a work of fiction. Similarities to real people, places, or events are entirely coincidental.

CONFLICT IN CONTENTION

First edition. January 13, 2024.

Copyright © 2024 Thomas 'DOC' Savage.

ISBN: 979-8224791019

Written by Thomas 'DOC' Savage.

CHAPTER ONE

In a secluded box canyon off the much larger Sabino Canyon, near the foot of the Santa Catalina Mountains, where desert and mountain meet, stands a stout cabin built of native stone. A covered porch across the front of that cabin holds two handcrafted rocking chairs. From that cabin, a man steps out and onto the porch. He is unremarkable. Neither tall nor short. Neither broad nor thin. He's just a man.

He is dressed all in black: pants, shirt, leather vest, boots - all black. On his head a broad-brimmed black hat. At his side a black gun belt holds a custom built .36 caliber cap and ball pistol with walnut grips much polished by use.

He steps off the porch and over to a ramada where a strange little man is busy at an outdoor stove. The little man's legs are bent at angles God never intended, and he moves in a weird, hopping motion.

"G'morning, Preacher," the small man calls.

"Morning, Budge," the man called Preacher answers. "How are you doing today?"

The question is asked sincerely. The man in black knows the struggles Budge endures because of the wounds he suffered during that cussed war where both his legs had been crushed when he was run over by a horse-drawn cannon. Those breaks couldn't be properly set and had healed into the configuration one saw today. Budge endured constant pain that was helped by laudanum to differing degrees, depending on the day.

"Doing good t'day, Preacher. Doing real good t'day."

Preacher had befriended and then rescued Budge when he had been considered Tucson's town drunk. Preacher had gotten Budge medical help, brought him to his own home where Budge had built himself an apartment. And he had turned out to be not just a first-class carpenter but a better-than-most cook.

As proof of that, Budge set two plates on a table containing light fluffy biscuits, bacon and eggs, plus cups of steaming coffee for both.

Since Preacher had rescued Budge and cleaned him up, and his talents had been discovered, every café and restaurant for miles around had tried to lure

Budge away. But the little man was fiercely loyal to the man who had brought him out of poverty and shame.

"Got any plans for t'day?" Budge asked.

"Yes, I'm gonna ride down to Tombstone to see Wyatt and Virgil, then swing west over to Contention. Got some business to take care of over there. Shouldn't take more than a day or so."

"Well, looks like a right fine day for a ride, but have a care. Ain't a whole lot of good ever came out of Contention."

* * * * *

In the stable behind the cabin, Preacher brushed his long-legged, deep chested Mustang, then gave close attention to each hoof before saddling up. Preacher had gotten the Mustang from an ancient Apache when the horse was but a colt. The old Indian had tried to explain the name the colt had been given, but the closest Preacher could come to the name was 'Jim.' But from the first, a deep bond had developed between the man and the horse. There weren't many horses around that could catch Jim in a quarter mile, and he had plenty of bottom and could run all day if necessary.

To complete this family, a huge Irish Wolfhound sat and watched as Preacher got his horse ready for the trail. His name was Dog, and he went an easy one-hundred-thirty pounds and could easily take down a full-grown timber wolf. Dog was every bit as loyal to Preacher as Jim was, having been rescued from under a burned-out wagon after an Indian attack. Barely weaned, Preacher had carried Dog home curled up inside his vest.

A strange family this was for certain, but far happier than most.

* * * * *

The trip from just north of Tucson to Tombstone was about one hindered and fifteen miles. Too much for a single day, so Preacher was wont to spend the night with a friend who lived in the little Mormon settlement of St. David. Up and off with the sunrise, he rode into Tombstone just after midday.

Since Preacher was a man nearly obsessed with cleanliness, as always, his first stop was at Sing Wan's Laundry for a hot bath and to have his clothes washed at the same time. Finally, rested and refreshed, he was seated at a table in the Rural Dining Hall near the end of Toughnut Street when two men in knee length black coats stepped inside.

All conversation ceased as the two men stood just inside the door for a moment to allow their eyes to adjust from the brilliant sunshine outside. Both men were tall and slim. Both sported huge walrus-style mustaches.

"Over here, Wyatt," Preacher called from his table in the corner. Preacher was seated with his back to the wall and where he could see both doors. But as the Earp brothers approached, he stood and moved to the other side, so the two lawmen could have that same advantage.

"Good to see you, Preacher," Wyatt said. "Been a while since you've been down this way."

"It has at that," Preacher replied. "And I'm just passing through as it is. Got some business over in Contention."

"Contention, huh? You watch yourself over there. Somebody ought to burn that place to the ground. Ain't nothing there but the scum of the Earth, seems like."

"I'm afraid you're right, old friend. But I've been hired by a man who thinks his young son is there and tied up with some bad people. He wants me to see if I can locate him and get him outta there. I suppose I can take a look around without ruffling anybody's tail feathers too much. How about you? Keeping things under control here in Tombstone?"

Wyatt accepted a mug of hot coffee from a serving girl and said, "Aw, same old thing. The McLaury boys are cutting up some. I'll most likely have to dent their heads to get their attention."

Virgil spoke up to say, "It's that Frank. Tom would settle down and do right, but Frank keeps him worked up."

About then, plates loaded with huge beef steaks and fried potatoes were set before them, and the old friends spent a leisurely hour or so catching up and rehashing old times.

All too soon, the lawmen had to get back to work, so Preacher walked with them as far as the Oriental Hotel where he intended to get a good night's sleep and head for Contention early the next day.

CHAPTER TWO

Preacher left Tombstone as the sun was just beginning to clear the Dragoon Mountains. He put that sun at his back and rode cross-country toward the hard-bitten town of Contention and the job he had been hired to do. As he rode, a mockingbird serenaded him from atop a late blooming Palo Verde tree.

Jim, his Mustang, was eager for the trail and moved along at a fast walk that ate up miles as Dog, the massive Wolfhound, trotted alongside. Preacher tipped his hat to a group of Chiricahua Apache women who were using long poles to harvest Saguaro fruit.

When the sun was directly overhead, he came upon the lawless town he had been bidden to go to. He stopped before entering to look the situation over, as he had never had reason to visit the place before.

Using the binoculars he'd been issued as a sniper for the Army of the Confederacy, he slowly examined the scene before him. For such a small village, he was surprised to count no less than five saloons. There were three scattered along the west side of the single street and two on the east side. There were two cafes, a small two-story hotel, a combination livery and blacksmith shop, a general store, and a hardware store that advertised 'guns bought, sold, and repaired.'

Six or seven small buildings may have been homes, and one burned-out shell with metal bars rising from blackened timbers spoke of where a jail had once stood.

He saw at least a dozen saddle horses standing at hitching rails outside various buildings and one buckboard in front of the general store. Men in range clothes were seated at benches along a boardwalk or wandering from saloon to saloon. With the exception of the burned-out jail, it was not unlike a hundred other small frontier towns. Only its reputation set it apart.

He kneed Jim forward and rode slowly down the center of the town's single street, gathering curious glances from the men on the boardwalks. He acknowledged the looks with a slight nod of his head and dismounted at the livery stable. A man in soot-stained denims stood at an anvil, swinging a hammer against a brightly glowing horseshoe. He dropped the shoe in a tub of water and came over to where Preacher was stepping down from the saddle. He looked Preacher over from head to foot before speaking

"Stranger, are ya? Whatcha need?" About then, Dog stepped inside the livery from where he had been relieving himself against the side of the building. When Dog sat down beside Jim, the smith blew out his breath in surprise. "Lord a'mighty, but that's one ugly dog, if it even *is* a dog. Kin I pet 'im?"

"Sure," Preacher answered, "if you don't mind losing a few fingers, that is. He don't take kindly to being touched."

The smith had already started forward with his hand outstretched, but when Preacher spoke, he quickly stepped backward. "Uh, yeah, alright then. What kin I do fer ya?"

"I'd like a stall for my horse and dog and a bit of oats for the horse. If the dog gets hungry, I suppose he'll just catch himself a rat or two. I might be in town a day or so."

"Sure, sure, I kin do that. Got business here, do ya?"

"My own, yes," Preacher answered. He removed a silver dollar from his pocket and handed it to the livery man who made it disappear as if by magic. Preacher turned his back and stepped out into the street.

He had a detailed description of the kid he was looking for, so he figured to start visiting saloons until he found him. The first one he came to was called the Red Dog Saloon. He pushed the doors open and walked inside, and then stepped to the side so he could let his eyes adjust to the dimness inside after the bright sun of the street. It was a small place with a bar across the back wall, a mirror behind the bar, and half a dozen tables with mismatched chairs scattered around the floor.

Three men stood at the bar and two more were seated at one of the tables playing cards. They all looked up when he stepped inside. One of the men at the bar was an absolute brute. All of six feet tall and half as broad. He had a battered face that looked like he had fallen out of an Ugly Tree and hit every branch on the way down. He pushed himself away from the bar and stepped over to where Preacher stood. The body odor that rolled off the man nearly made Preacher's eyes water.

"We don't cotton to strangers 'round here, so why don't you…?" Then the big man looked down at the gun at Preacher's hip and said, "Well, would you look at that? You don't even carry a real gun! Got one of them old timey cap and ball things. Lemme see that."

He reached his big hand, fingers thick as sausages, for the gun and in a flash, Preacher pulled the pistol and stuck the tip of the barrel in the big man's nostril.

"Sorry, pard, but I don't let nobody handle my gun."

With that, he pushed the gun deeper into the big man's nose, and the man had to step back. Then as quick as he had drawn it, the pistol was back in the holster.

A startled expression passed over the big man's face. "Whoa!" he said. "That was like *magic*! Yer sure enough fast with that thing, mister. C'mon and lemme buy ya a drink."

"Sure," Preacher answered. Without taking his eyes off the big man's face, he said to the barkeep, "I'll have a beer. Is it cold?"

"Yer darn tootin' it's cold," the bartender answered. "Got a big icehouse right out back." He drew a frothy glass and set it in front of Preacher who tasted it and, yes, it was very cold.

The big man ordered the same and lifted the glass toward Preacher. "I'm Biggie Hunter. That fast gun of your'n come with a name?"

"Sure. I'm...Bill Rooney," Preacher invented. "Thanks for the beer. Got some business here in town."

"Well, welcome t' Contention, Bill Rooney." With that, Biggie poured the contents of his glass down his throat and wiped his mouth with the back of his hand. "Let's have another'n," he said to the bartender.

"I'll just work on this one for a bit," Preacher said. "But you can tell me a little about this town. I've never been here before."

So, the man now known as Bill Rooney sat at a table with his new best friend, Biggie, to nurse his beer and pump the big guy for information.

"I reckon you seed the jail when ya come into town? That means there ain't no law in Contention. But that don't mean there ain't no rules. See, what we got is a Boss, and what The Boss says goes! And if ya don't like it, ya kin just rattle yer hocks back where ya come from." Biggie paused to drain off half of his second mug of beer before he continued.

"Them rules are pretty simple. The Boss says ya cain't bother none of the businesses here in town. And if ya kills somebody, ya gotta bury 'em. And if ya got a posse after ya, ya cain't come in 'til ya shake 'em."

"Sounds reasonable," Bill Rooney answered. "Who is this Boss you're talking about?"

"Well, Bill, it's like this. If The Boss wants ta see ya, then ya'll see The Boss. Elsewise, The Boss don't need ta be bothered."

"Fair enough," Bill Rooney said. "But look here, I come here looking for a friend. A young guy. Slim, average height, pale blonde hair. It almost looks white. Seen him?"

"Sorry, Bill," Biggie said, "but here in Contention, if somebody wants ta see ya, they'll find ya. Elsewise, ya don't ask no questions. Get it?"

"Yeah, I get it. In that case, I think I'll have a look around, see if I can find him. Thanks for the beer."

Bill Rooney stood up and walked out, leaving most of the beer behind. Biggie Hunter quickly picked up Bill's abandoned glass and drained it.

* * * * *

Preacher, now known as Bill Rooney, stepped out of the Red Dog Saloon and looked up the boardwalk to the next drinking spot. The sign hanging above the door proclaimed it to be the Two-Bit Saloon. He turned left and started that way.

The Two-Bit Saloon was a much classier place than the Red Dog. The bar along the right wall was of highly polished walnut. A life-sized, modest painting of a nude lady hung behind the bar.

Four wagon wheel chandeliers with six oil lamps each hung over the floor, making it much brighter inside. Eight tables with four chairs each stood around the floor. Half the tables were occupied, and five men stood at the bar.

Against the far wall stood a piano where a bald man with sleeve garters was beating out a lively tune. Beside him, on a tall chair, sat a man with a huge drooping mustache who held a ten-gauge double-barreled shotgun on his lap. Apparently, he was there to ensure order was observed.

Bill Rooney went to the bar and ordered a beer. It, too, was ice cold. Must be more than one icehouse in town. As the bartender set the beer in front of him, Bill repeated his request for information about his pale-haired, slender friend.

The bartender wore a neatly trimmed red beard and had a fringe of red hair around his head. His pink scalp was so shiny it looked polished. "Mayhap I've seen someone like that around time and again. Where he'd be right now, I have no idea. Mayhap he'll hear you're looking, and he'll find you. Or not. Who knows?" With that, he walked away, polishing the bar as he went.

Bill Rooney turned to lean his back against the bar and took a good look at the men scattered around the floor. Several of them wore suits of broadcloth, possibly businessmen. Two of them wore the flashier clothing of professional gamblers. The others were all dressed like cowhands. Maybe they even were. But none of them had pale blonde hair.

He went back outside, leaving the full glass of beer on the bar. The last saloon on this side of the street was called the Silver Dollar, and he headed that way.

As he approached the saloon, someone stepped quickly out of a doorway, wrapped their arms tightly around him so he couldn't move, and swung him into an empty alley. Preacher struggled against the grip that kept his arms pinned to his sides as his attacker slammed him viciously against the wall, knocking his breath out.

With the same move, the attacker grabbed Preacher's throat in a crushing grip and leaned close to whisper in his ear. "Alright, mister, who are you, and what do you want with the kid?"

As Preacher struggled to get his breath back, the attacker swung his other fist brutally into Preacher's midsection, further depriving him of needed oxygen.

Preacher tried to double over, but the grip on his throat held him against the wall. With the little air he had left, he gasped, "Rooney. I'm... Bill Rooney. What do you want?" Fortunately, he recalled his phony name.

"What I *want* is to know why you're asking questions about the boss's son?" the lips next to his ear whispered, just before slamming the other fist into his belly again. With that blow, the grip on his throat released, and Preacher dropped, gasping, to the ground.

Trying desperately to drag air into his lungs, Preacher looked up at his attacker, but the sun was directly behind him. All he could see was the outline of a big man in a wide-brimmed hat.

"No," Preacher gasped. "The kid I'm looking for is from Missouri, St... Lo... Louis."

The bulky figure above him kicked out viciously, catching Preacher in the hip and growled, "Get outta Contention, and don't come back. Or next time, I won't be so nice!"

After his attacker had left, Preacher struggled to his feet and shook his clothes back into some kind of order. It took a few minutes before he could stand erect, and when he did, his hip spasmed so that he nearly went back down again.

Eventually, he was able to make his way out of the alley and back onto the boardwalk. Looking both ways, he saw that nobody was paying any attention to him, so he limped his painful way to the hotel and asked for a room overlooking the street. He signed the register as Bill Rooney and made his way to the stairs.

He limped up the stairs to his room and went in. Standing with his back against the door, he looked carefully around. It was like a hundred other hotel rooms he'd been in. A double bed with a surprisingly comfortable mattress, a bowl and ewer on a small table, and a window that looked out onto the town.

He took the chair from the small table and wedged it under the doorknob before going to the window and pulling back the gauzy curtains. The street outside was quiet. A few men walked the boardwalk, intent on their own business. A buckboard loaded with supplies rolled slowly down the street. Shadows crept across the street as the sun sank low behind the hotel.

He stripped off his shirt and boots, washed as well as he could in the bowl, and dropped onto the bed where he soon fell into a deep sleep.

CHAPTER THREE

Preacher awoke to bright morning sunshine flooding through the window of his hotel room. His throat was dry and sore from nearly being crushed, and there was a black bruise on his right hip that he could not cover with both hands. There was a bone-deep ache there that caused him to move with a bit of a limp. He quickly washed and dressed before going downstairs.

Directly beside the hotel was a café called the Longhorn Café. It was so close, in fact, that a door had been cut into the hotel wall allowing access to the café from the lobby. He stepped through that door, and the first thing he saw was a stuffed and mounted head of a longhorn steer with the biggest horns he'd ever seen. There was a span of wall over eight feet from one tip of the horns to the other. He was instantly struck with how strong that steer would have to have been, just to hold up those majestic horns.

The next thing he saw was that every table was in use. He stood there looking around for a moment and saw a man at a table in the back waving at him. Preacher started walking that way and saw the man sat alone at a table for four and was inviting Preacher to join him.

The man was dressed in farmer's clothes and said, "Saw you looking at them horns. Really something, ain't they? Heard some say it'd take a buzzard half an hour to fly from one tip to t'other. Howdy! I'm Wayne Young. New in town, are you? Don't believe I've ever seen you before."

"Howdy, Wayne. I'm, uh, I'm Bill Rooney. Just in town hunting up an old friend."

Preacher looked his tablemate over as he sat down and had to admit this Wayne Young was one of the most handsome men he had ever seen. Every aspect of his face, from his thick, curly black hair to his full lips, came together to create a face worthy of a Greek god. And he noticed the waitresses circulating about the room were casting lingering glances at the man as well.

"Yeah, I heard that. And listen, I gotta tell you, nothing stays secret in Contention for long. But you need to know, asking the wrong question of the wrong person can be downright hazardous to your health."

"Yeah," Preacher remarked, "I sorta found that out yesterday." He unconsciously rubbed at his aching neck as he spoke.

One of the waitresses brought coffee to Preacher and allowed her fingers to trail casually over Wayne's shoulder as she left. Wayne didn't even glance at her. Instead, he said, "Well, look. You seem like a right nice feller, and I'd hate to see you come to grief. I gotta farm just four miles out of town, and I'm on my way there in just a minute. Why not ride out that way for supper. I can maybe tell you enough about the town to keep you from getting killed. And besides, I'd be proud to have you meet my wife. She's just the prettiest thing in five states!"

Preacher thought, 'Well, it stands to reason, a guy this good looking would have an equally good-looking wife.' "Sure, Wayne. That sounds like a plan. I guess I didn't know what I'd be getting into here and seems like I've upset some folks already. I'll see you out there come midday."

Wayne Young gave Preacher directions to his farm, then rose and left. Every female in the room watched him with admiring eyes as he went out.

* * * * *

The sun was high and shadows were small when Preacher rode through the gate to Wayne Young's neat farm. The dooryard was clean and swept, and a dozen or so chickens scratched in the shade of the frame-built two-story farmhouse. A large barn and smaller tool shed stood behind the house, and all the buildings wore a fresh coat of paint, a rarity in western places.

Wayne himself was shirtless and swinging an axe at the roots of a huge mesquite stump. That stump looked near as big as a buffalo bull. Preacher rode up and stepped down from the saddle, leaving Jim ground hitched. Dog sat down beside the Mustang, prepared to wait as long as the man needed.

The roots of dead mesquite trees can be hard as iron. This was no exception, and the stump was massive. Wayne stood and arched his back to stretch it, but Preacher took off his gun belt and hung it from the saddle horn, followed it with his shirt, picked up a shovel, and began digging to expose more of the roots. Not a word was spoken. Wayne took up his axe again and went back to chopping at the exposed roots. The axe was sharp, but the roots would not give up easily.

After a while, they traded tools. Wayne took the shovel and Preacher, now Bill Rooney, took the axe. Back to work they went. After another half hour, the final root was severed, and the stump rolled free. The two men stood up straight and stretched their spines again. Wayne finally spoke.

"My wife's been wanting to put a flower bed here, but I swear it'd have taken me the rest of the day to grub this stump out if you hadn't helped out."

About then, a sweet voice called from inside the house. "Honey, come get washed up. Lunch's ready. Bring your friend."

The two men collected their shirts and walked to the front door where a basin stood on a bench with a clean towel hanging beside it. With the sweat and dirt washed from his face and his wavy hair finger-combed, Wayne again looked like an Adonis, and said to Preacher, "C'mon, let's go in. I'm anxious for you to meet my lovely wife."

Together they trooped inside where the wife was waiting. Wayne swept his arms around her and lifted her off her feet to swing her around. As he set her back down, he said, "Honey, this here is Bill Rooney. Just met him today."

Preacher tried hard not to let his shock show on his face. The woman standing before him with her hand outstretched to shake was maybe five feet tall and twenty pounds overweight. Her face was cute, with pink apple cheeks and sparkling blue eyes, a tiny pug nose, and unremarkable lips. She was comely to be sure, but compared to the classic beauty of her husband, she was nothing to write home about. And yet, to Wayne, she was obviously gorgeous.

A line from somewhere came into Preacher's mind; 'Beauty is in the eyes of the beholder.' Obviously, that was what he was seeing here, and the two people before him were obviously as happy together as they could possibly be.

Preacher took the proffered hand and bowed slightly over it. "It's a pleasure to meet such a lovely lady."

She beamed a smile and made a dismissive wave with her other hand, saying, "Come into the kitchen, you two. Lunch is ready."

Lunch was delicious fried chicken, oven-baked potatoes, and fresh corn on the cob. Both men ate until they could eat no more. And then Belinda, that was Wayne's wife's name, cleared the dishes off the table and set in their place a hot, fresh peach pie. The men looked at each other, and as one, loosened their belts and prepared to do justice to this wonderful dessert.

* * * * *

Later, as the dying sun painted the few, wispy clouds in brilliant reds and golds and as the stars began their nightly show, Preacher and Wayne Young relaxed on the porch, savoring a last cup of coffee. Their conversation turned to the outlaw village of Contention.

"The whole shebang," Wayne said, "is run by the guy they call The Boss. Like as not, you'll never see him. Most folks don't, nor do you want to. The less you know about him, the better. But believe me, he'll know all there is to know about you. Now, this guy you say you're looking for; quit looking. By now, everybody already knows why you're in town. So just relax and let him come to you. Folks get a mite antsy when someone starts asking questions, this being an outlaw town and all.

"If this feller wants to see you, he will find you, in his time. Just find yourself a comfortable spot and wait. If he don't show up, then you're just wasting your time and might as well go on to something else. I just got a feeling you're too good a feller to get yourself killed for being too inquisitive.

"Now, Belinda and I been farming here for nigh onto eight years, and we get all our supplies, mail, and such outta Contention. But we don't bother nobody there, and nobody bothers us. You take that tack, and you'll do alright."

"Yeah, I understand. And I sure appreciate you telling me. But I reckon I best be getting back. Please tell your wife…"

"Oh, nothing of the kind. It's late, and we got three empty bedrooms upstairs. We always figured on having a whole passel of young'uns, but I reckon it ain't to be. So, no sense in you traipsing all the way back to town when there's a bed up there waiting for you. And Belinda will fix us a better breakfast than you can get in town, come morning."

Preacher replied, "Well, I sure can't turn down an offer like that, now, can I?"

By the time the moon came up, the lights went out in that trim, little farmhouse, and peace reigned.

CHAPTER FOUR

Back in Contention, Preacher took the advice of his new friend, Wayne Young, and took the time to check out the two saloons on the east side of the street. Directly across the street from the hotel was the Blue Moon Saloon. It consisted of a plain wooden bar across the back wall with seven tables crowding the floor. The tables and chairs were crowded together, because nearly half the floor was set aside for dancing. A battered piano stood against the wall in the cleared space, and two guitars stood beside it. Preacher dismissed this place at once, knowing that when the dancing started, any chance for a quiet conversation would disappear.

The last place was at the south end of the street with nothing beyond it but sagebrush and cactus. It was a Mexican style cantina and looked like a place where a man could think. The sign hanging above the door simply read Cantina and inside, smells of south-of-the-border cooking comingled with the scents of cigarette tobacco and spilled beer.

Bottles of yellowish mescal and clear tequila stood behind the bar, and a sign in English and Spanish proclaimed cold beer was on tap for ten cents a glass. Two men stood at the bar. One in cowboy duds; the other dressed like a vaquero in tight, flared britches, a waist length jacket, and a huge sombrero hanging by a cord down his back.

Preacher decided this would be the place where Bill Rooney would wait to see if the blonde-haired boy he was looking for would find him. He approached the barkeeper and said, "Hola, amigo. Una cerveza, por favor." He was proficient with the language, although rusty since he hadn't had much occasion to use it lately. Maybe that would change while he was here.

He collected his beer, left a dime on the bar, and walked to a table that stood beside a window looking out onto the street. A deck of cards lay on the table, and he picked them up to idly shuffle through them. As he did that, the two from the bar walked over to him, and the cowboy asked, "How about a game?"

Preacher took in the two with a glance and saw nothing untoward in either. Just two bored men looking to pass some time. "Sure. Have a seat. I'm Bill Rooney. Who are you?"

The cowboy introduced himself as Mickey Dunn, and the Mexican was Pedro Gonzales. In a different life, Preacher could have been a gambler. He knew most of their tricks and wiles. But he was satisfied that the two with him now weren't any kind of card sharps, so they just played four-card-draw through the afternoon. No blonde kid showed up before Preacher called the game to have some of the great smelling food that was being prepared in the back room.

* * * * *

After eating, Preacher wandered down to the stable where he gave Jim a good rubdown and spent some time scratching Dog's wiry coat before returning to the Cantina where he waited until midnight. No blonde lad showed up, so he walked across the street to the hotel and went to bed.

* * * * *

Preacher followed the same procedure for the next two days. Mickey Dunn and Pedro Gonzales showed up both days to continue their poker game. They were both enthusiastic but terrible players, and Preacher finally realized he was winning way too much of their money. So, he began folding winning hands just to try to preserve their finances. By the end of the second day, he decided he had spent enough time in this fruitless pursuit. If this kid wanted to get ahold of him, he surely would have done so by now.

He saddled Jim by the light of a full moon and rode slowly out of town. He was looking forward to getting back to Tombstone and a hot bath and then Tucson and his own snug home. He'd just have to tell his client that the kid didn't want to be found.

He was about to pass the last building on the north end of the street when a man stepped directly in front of him. He either had to pull Jim to a panic stop or run the man down. Preacher didn't use a steel bit in Jim's mouth, just a soft hackamore. He pulled Jim's nose sharply down to stop him, but the horse had already anticipated the command and was sliding to a stop.

"What the heck, mister? You trying to get yourself killed?" Preacher barked at the stranger in front of him.

The man just stood there; his face lost in the moon shadow from his broad black hat. He spoke low, "The Boss wants to see you."

Preacher shrugged. Just when he thought he had a cold case, now it heats up. "Alright. Lead the way," he said.

The man crossed the street and took the alley beside the Silver Dollar Saloon. He went to the rear of the building and stopped beside a back door. "In here," he said.

Preacher dropped Jim's reins beside a Palo Verde tree where there was a small patch of dried grass, dismounted, and followed the dark man through the door and up two flights of stairs.

His guide pushed a door open but remained outside. "In here," he said again.

Preacher stepped inside the room where he saw a table and someone seated at the far side. There were two lamps on the table, and they both had reflectors behind them, so the light was all cast at him and not the person behind the table who remained in shadow. Preacher could vaguely make out that there was someone behind the person seated at the table but wasn't able to see either one clearly.

There was no chair on his side of the table, so all he could do was stand there and wait. Finally, the person behind the lights spoke. "Who are you?" The voice was neutral with no inflections or accent.

"Name's Bill Rooney," Preacher responded.

"Why are you here?"

"Looking for a kid. His father wants to know if he's alright."

There was silence for a few seconds from behind the table and then a faint tearing sound was followed by, "The kid doesn't want to talk to you or his father."

"Then I guess we have nothing to discuss," Preacher answered and turned toward the door he had come in through.

There was another faint tearing sound, and the voice spoke again, "Wait a minute."

"Why"" Preacher answered. "If the kid doesn't want to talk, we've got nothing more to say."

There was faint, whispered conversation from behind the lights for a few seconds, then the voice responded, "You say you're from the boy's father. How is he?"

"Funny thing. He was thought to have cholera when the boy was taken, but he's getting better now, so…"

More whispering, then, "Are you sure it was cholera?"

"The doctors are never sure about anything, but cholera was what they suspected. But that was, what? Ten days ago? Last I heard, he was still alive."

After more whispering, the voice commanded, "You may go, but do not leave town."

"Now just a doggone minute here. I came here to talk to a kid. I don't know who you are, but if that kid don't want to talk to me, I have no reason to stay in this fleabag town. I already been beaten and kicked. Now I've got better places to be."

After more whispering, the voice spoke in a much more conciliatory tone, "I'm asking politely if you will remain in town one more day?"

Preacher hesitated for a moment, then answered, "Alright. Since you asked politely, I'll stay one more day. But by midnight tomorrow, I have other places to be."

The people hiding behind the lights stood up and walked away. Preacher did the same and went back down the stairs and outside. The dark man was waiting there beside Jim and Dog.

"I'll take care of your animals," he said.

"No thanks," Preacher said. "I'll see to them myself."

Stepping into the saddle, he returned to the livery stable where he put up his animals again and then returned to the hotel where he reregistered for his room and went to bed.

CHAPTER FIVE

On the third floor above the Silver Dollar Saloon, a lovely, auburn-haired woman in a bright green, form-fitting dress entered a room where a tow-haired young man was lying on a bed. The lad's face was bright red with fever, and his nearly white hair was slicked with sweat. Sheets and blankets from the bed had been kicked to the floor.

The woman approached the bed. A small-framed man started to follow, and then, based on the conversation they'd just had, he hung back apprehensively.

The woman laid a dainty hand on the boy's burning forehead and spoke softly, "Cholera. How could it be cholera?"

She turned back to where the small man was inching slowly toward the door. "How could it be cholera? Didn't Rooney say William was getting better?"

"Yes, Boss. That's what he said. But how can you trust the word of some drifting saddle tramp?"

"Send someone to Tombstone and get the best doctor in town. Bring him here at gunpoint if they have to. But tell them it's cholera and to bring the best medicine they have. Hurry now."

"Sure, Boss, right away, but...don't they say there is no cure for cholera? Isn't that what they say?"

"I don't care what they say. I want my son to live. It's taken me this long to get him here, I can't stand the thought of losing him now. Not like this. Hurry!"

The small man rushed gratefully from the sick room.

* * * * *

The rider who had been dispatched to Tombstone was able to ride easily through the night. The light of the full moon made the landscape nearly as bright as day. But as he rode, his thoughts kept time with the drumming of his horse's hooves...cholera, cholera, cholera. Finally, he came to a decision and turned his horse from east to due north and rode instead toward far-off Benson. He wanted nothing to do with cholera. Nothing at all.

* * * * *

When Preacher rose in the morning, he was feeling considerably better about the task that had brought him here. He washed and dressed and went downstairs for breakfast. But as he stepped into the café, he found the place in a state of confusion.

Mae, the cute young serving girl, was running back and forth between the café floor and the kitchen. As she raced past him, she hurriedly said, "I can bring you coffee in just a bit and some biscuits in a few minutes. I had to make them myself, so I don't know how good they'll be. Hector, the cook, quit this morning. Seems he was hired to replace the cook over at the Silver Dollar who came down sick with something. I'll be with you as soon as I can."

He took a seat, and she soon set a cup of coffee in front of him, slopping much of it on the table in her haste. Eventually, she brought him a plate containing two biscuits and a dab of butter. They weren't bad, but you couldn't call them good, either. But it was food and it satisfied his appetite.

As he walked down the street to check on Jim and Dog, he happened to notice the hardware store was still closed and locked, the shade still drawn over the window in the door. Something must be keeping the owner away.

When he arrived at the stables, the blacksmith and livery keeper weren't there either. In fact, there were very few people out and about on the streets as well. He wondered briefly what was going on but soon forgot about it as he fed and brushed his Mustang and spent a few minutes with Dog before heading across the street to the Cantina. At least his poker partners were in their usual places.

He ordered his beer and took a seat at the table by the window and prepared to spend another day waiting.

* * * * *

As the day wore on, Preacher was surprised at how little activity there was on the street. In fact, he spotted two young boys, brothers by the looks of them, busily occupied with something they had found out there in the street. He'd seen a few youngsters in town, but for the most part they stayed on the fringes.

But these two were right out in the street. Preacher rose up a mite in his chair to see what they were doing.

What he saw was a huge tarantula. It looked near as big as a man's glove. The boys had sticks and were poking at it from a safe distance. The huge spider was standing as tall as it could on six pairs of legs and waving the other pair threateningly at the boys, trying to frighten them into leaving him alone. They showed no sign of being frightened.

But one of those boys lifted his eyes to glance down the street. Then he shook his brother's shoulder, pointed down the street, and both dropped their sticks, forgot about the spider, and disappeared down an alley.

Preacher looked that way to see what had spooked them and saw three men, spread out across the street and walking slowly his way. When the three were twenty yards from the cantina door, they stopped, and one of them hollered, "Rooney! Get out here! We aim ta kill ya!"

Through the window, Preacher studied each man. He was certain he had never seen any of them before.

Mickey Dunn was also looking out the window at the three men who all had Colts slung low on their hips. "What did you do to rile them folks up?" he asked Preacher.

"Can't rightly say," Preacher answered. "Don't believe I've ever seen them before."

"Huh! Well, you ain't planning on going out there, are you?"

"Reckon I'll have to. Can't stay here in the cantina forever."

"But there's three of 'em! Look, if you're going out there, I'm going with you. How about you, Pedro?"

"Of course, Señor Mickey. Three against one no is fair. Not at all."

Preacher rose from his chair and settled his pistol on his hip. "Thanks for that, fellas, but this isn't your fight. You stay right here. I'll go see what they want. Maybe this is all a mistake." He walked to the door and stepped out onto the boardwalk.

Mickey and Pedro stepped out right behind him. Preacher turned to place his hand on Mickey's chest. "No! I appreciate the support, but you're not involved in this. Stay here!" With that, he stepped down to the street, walked out to the middle of the dusty road, and turned to face the trio before him.

None of the men were familiar. But the one on the right and the one in the middle both had bright fever spots on their pale cheeks, and their faces ran with sweat. They appeared to be quite ill. The one on the left didn't have the same look of sickness on him, but he did look determined to take a life.

"What's this all about?" Preacher asked. "I don't know you gentlemen. Never seen any of you before."

"That don't matter none." The man in the middle hollered. "We know you! You're the varmint what brung cholera here. Now we're gonna die, but we're taking you with us. So, fill your hand!"

With that, all three went for their guns. But as it turned out, none of them were the gunmen they thought they were. In self-defense, Preacher had to draw his own pistol and pull the trigger. His first round took the man on the right directly through the heart, and he was blown backwards by the force of the shot. He stretched out full-length on his back and didn't move again.

His second shot came so quickly, the two shots sounded like one. That shot took the man in the middle right between the eyes, and he folded up like a puppet whose strings had been suddenly cut. That only left the man on the left side.

By now, he'd gotten his pistol out and was stabbing flame at where Preacher was standing just a split second ago. But as Preacher had triggered his second shot, he'd thrown himself to his left, landing on his side in the dust. From there, he triggered a third shot that struck the remaining gunman in the center of his chest. Blood blossomed on his shirt, but he didn't go down. He was even now swinging his pistol to where Preacher lay in the dirt of the street. But before that pistol could come to bear, Preacher fired a fourth time.

That shot also hit the standing man heart high. The gunman looked down at the hand that wouldn't obey him, then looked over to where Preacher was starting to rise. He opened his mouth as if to speak, but his knees collapsed, and he went forward on his face and didn't move again.

Preacher still stood with his pistol extended and swept his eyes over the three corpses laying at his feet. Mickey Dunn and Pedro Gonzalez stepped into the street beside Preacher. Mickey said, "Dang me if I ever saw anybody that fast with a gun! Who the heck are you, anyway?"

"Nobody," Preacher responded. "I'm just someone who didn't want to get killed today, that's all."

"Alright, Mr. 'Someone.' I'll go get a wagon. We gotta bury these guys," Pedro said.

CHAPTER SIX

While Preacher and Mickey Dunn waited for Pedro Gonzalez to return with a wagon, Preacher swapped the nearly empty cylinder in his pistol for a fully loaded one. He always carried two loaded cylinders in addition to the one already in his pistol and changing them out only took a few seconds.

Mickey watched as Preacher accomplished this task, then said, "I have never seen anybody draw and fire as fast as you just did. Nobody! So, who the heck are you, anyway? I mean, I was up in Deadwood one time and saw Hickock in action, and I thought *he* was fast. But even he wouldn't hold a candle to what I just saw. So, who *are* you?"

"I'm nobody, Mickey. Just a messenger, that's all.

"Oh, c'mon now! There ain't but maybe half a dozen men who are real gunfighters, and they're all well known. But I ain't never heard of no Bill Rooney."

"Well, I sure am not a gunfighter and don't care to be known as one. I'm just a man; just a messenger, that's all."

"Alright, alright, you don't want to be known. I get it. But what was that talk about cholera? He said you brought cholera here. That right? Do you know how dangerous that stuff is? Cholera's wiped out whole towns."

"Now, that's a puzzlement. The man who sent me here was said to have cholera but was getting over it. Besides, I never even saw the man. He hired me by telegram. Never had any contact with him. So, if there's cholera here, I didn't bring it."

Pedro arrived with the wagon. Mickey said, "Well, let's get these fellas loaded up," and walked over to where Pedro waited.

"Hold on there a bit," Preacher called after him. "Two of these men looked a mite peaked. You know, feverish? And since he mentioned cholera, maybe touching them isn't a good idea. I'll go over to the hotel and get some blankets to wrap them in first."

Preacher crossed the street to the hotel. A small crowd had gathered around the bodies, mostly young men. The word 'cholera' was mentioned, and the crowd took it up.

"Didja hear what he said?" one of the young men asked. "He said these here fellas had cholera! My brother died of that stuff! Don't get too close."

The small crowd stepped further away from the three dead men in the street. Then, one by one, they turned and left.

Preacher returned with three ratty, old blankets and together, using their boots as much as they could, got the bodies wrapped and laid them in the wagon.

Pedro leaned against the side of the wagon and said, "Maybe we should have searched them, see if they had any papers saying who they are. Were!"

"Yeah, maybe we should, "Mickey answered. "But the idea don't much appeal to me. How about you, Bill?"

"No, I don't cotton much to that idea neither. I'll just leave their hats on their graves so folks that know them will know which is which."

They climbed up on the wagon seat, and Pedro drove slowly to the town cemetery.

* * * * *

Inside the Silver Dollar Saloon, a beautiful, auburn-haired woman in a bright green dress sat at a table near the polished bar with a glass of red wine in front of her. She tapped impatiently on the rim of the glass with long, polished fingernails. "Where is that cussed doctor? He should have been here long ago! Dutch!" she called to the large, bald man behind the bar, "Dutch, send another rider to Tombstone to get a doctor. Send one to Fort Huachuca, too. Quickly! We have to get a doctor here for James!"

The barkeeper hurried from the room, and the lady went back to nervously tapping the wine glass with her fingernails. It had taken her far too long to get her son here, she couldn't lose him now! She just couldn't!

* * * * *

In his hotel room, Preacher carefully reloaded his partly empty pistol cylinder with premeasured paper cartridges and conical bullets. Then, he disassembled the pistol and placed the barrel in a basin of hot, soapy water. He ran a small copper brush several times through the bore. Black powder can gum up a barrel almighty fast and have a terrible effect on accuracy. When he was convinced the lands and grooves were as clean as a whistle, he reassembled the weapon, lightly oiled each part, and returned the pistol to his holster.

Finally, he wedged a chair under the doorknob, blew out the light, and went to sleep. The fact that he had sent three men to the Promised Land affected him not in the least. They had given him no choice.

* * * * *

On the top floor of the Silver Dollar Saloon, in a small room, a tow-haired young man thrashed about in a welter of sheets and blankets. He was burning up with fever but shivered violently, as if he was freezing. His tortured guts clenched and unclenched viciously but there was nothing in them to come out. Not even stomach bile. In his agony, he whimpered like a hurt puppy.

* * * * *

Lonny Johnson was trying hard to stand at attention, even though he was no soldier, had never been a soldier, and had no interest in being a soldier. But he was standing before the desk of one Captain Ezekiel Dyer. (Zeke to his friends. He had very few friends.) The man was the very image of a military officer. His uniform was spanking clean and sharply pressed. His sandy hair cut short and face shaved clean, with the exception of a cavalry mustache.

Captain Dyer was seated behind a plain wooden desk that held nothing but an inkwell and a pen. His hazel eyes were drilling into Lonny Johnson as if he were something disgusting he had found stuck to one of his highly polished boots.

"Contention? Are you out of your mind, boy?" Dyer barked the words as if they were somehow distasteful to him. "Why in the name of all that's holy would I ever consent to going to that hell-hole?"

Lonny Johnson was trying hard to remain standing there with his head up, shoulders back, and feet together. But he constantly had to re-adjust his feet to keep from falling on his face.

"Sir, it's The Boss's son. He's powerful sick, might as well die if you won't come help 'im, Sir. They say he got the cholera, Sir."

"Don't be ridiculous. There hasn't been a case of cholera here in twenty years!" Captain Dyer dismissed Johnson's assessment of the situation.

"But, Captain, Sir, Your Honor, he didn't get the cholera here. He already had it when the Boss kidna... uh, picked 'im up down Natchez way. He 'as already sick when he got here. Sir."

"Natchez, you say? Well, sure, in that heat and humidity, cholera does show up on occasion. But look here! I am the Company Surgeon here at Fort Huachuca. I can't go traipsing off to that nest of outlaws and malcontents. No, no, it's out of the question."

"But you gotta come, your honor, Sir. He'll die 'less you do. And the Boss will, will...well I don't rightly know *what* The Boss'd do if James dies, but it'd be plumb awful. I know it would. You gotta come. Your honor, Sir! Please!"

Captain Ezekiel Dyer leaned back in his chair, crossed his arms on his chest, his chin resting in one hand, and regarded the ragged specimen that stood wobbling before him.

"Well," he mused out loud, "we don't presently have any patrols out where someone may be injured. And I suppose if an outbreak should occur out in that hellhole, it might well spread to other places. Oh, very well. Let me get some supplies together. Give me five minutes, then get your horse and meet me out front."

"But Captain, Sir, I most near run my horse to death to get here. He'd never stand the trip back. Sir."

"What? Of all the ignorant...alright, I'll have the quartermaster issue you a new mount. Just get out of my office while I get ready."

Lonny Johnson exhaled loudly as he sagged down into a more natural, for him, stance, and turning, scurried out of the surgeon's office like a rat released from a cage.

* * * * *

'Too Tall' Edwards was a strange-looking individual. Over six and a half feet tall but weighing less than one-hundred-forty pounds, he epitomized the image of Ichabod Crane. His oversized head perched atop a long and thin neck with an Adam's apple sticking out like an appendage. His legs were so long that his stirrups couldn't be let down far enough. Mounted, he always looked like a jockey on a racehorse with his knees drawn up near his horse's neck.

Too Tall was currently riding swiftly toward Tombstone in hopes of convincing a doctor to accompany him to Contention to treat The Boss's son. As he reached the point where the previous rider had turned away from the trail and lit a shuck for Benson, he also had a brief moment when he considered the possibility of abandoning this quest and saving himself instead. But something in his nature made him as faithful as he was gawky. He pressed on.

When he arrived in Tombstone, Too Tall quickly stepped off his horse and hurried up the stairs that ran beside the newspaper office. He knew from previous experience that one of the best doctors in town had his office up there.

At the top of the stairs, he burst into the office without knocking and startled the doctor who was seated behind his desk reading a new copy of the Epitaph.

"Doc, ya gotta come with me. There's a young man like to die unless you come!"

"Die? Where's this youngster at?" Doctor Willis asked as he jumped to his feet.

"Over in Contention, Doc. We gotta hurry. He's powerful sick, he is."

"Contention?" Willis spit the word out as though it had a bad taste. "Why you consarned idiot! I'd no more go to Contention than I'd go to Hades if I had a choice, and I do! Get out of my office!"

"But Doc! Ya gotta come. He's The Boss's only son, and he might die."

"Well, let him! Let that whole miserable town die and blow away. No, sir! Get outta my office, or I'll call the Earps. Get, now! Get!"

Doctor Willis rose from behind his desk and advanced on Too Tall, brandishing a brass-headed cane like a sword.

Too Tall was loyal but not stupid. He turned and hurried from the office and back down the stairs. Now where was he going to find a doctor? He ducked into the newspaper office and found a young printer's devil behind a counter, his shirt and hands deeply stained with ink.

"Where can I find a doctor?" Too Tall asked the young man.

"Why, that ain't so hard. Just go up the stairs. He's right there."

"No, not him. He already said no. I need another doc."

"Oh, well, in that case, there's Doctor McCloon, over on Fifth Street. He's…"

But Too Tall was already gone. He didn't even bother taking his horse. With his long legs, he could run near as fast as the horse anyway.

Doctor McCloon's office was on the ground floor, but that doctor chased him out, just as the first one had, as soon as he mentioned Contention.

What was he going to do now? There wasn't another doctor in town! Morosely, he walked back to his horse and mounted up. Where could he go? He'd move a mountain for The Boss if he was asked, but he couldn't invent a doctor. With no other idea in mind, he pointed his horse to the southeast and headed for Bisbee, twenty-five miles away. He had to find someone to help.

CHAPTER SEVEN

Next morning, the sun came up like a young lion out of a den, eager to find something to kill. The coolness of evening vanished in an instant as that sun rose into the cloudless, blue bowl of sky that stretched from horizon to horizon. The temperature on the valley floor would soon reach triple digits.

Preacher walked into the Café to find things running more smoothly. Mae, the serving girl, wasn't nearly as harried. "G'mornin'," she said in greeting as Preacher took a seat. "We got an old feller used to be a chuckwagon cook tending to the kitchen today. He's not bad, so what kin I getcha?"

"Coffee and a couple hotcakes?" Preacher answered.

"Cooky's making sourdough flapjacks. Will that do?"

"Sounds good," he responded, and she hurried off to fetch the coffee.

The flapjacks, when they arrived, weren't bad. With a liberal application of prickly pear syrup, they were right tasty. Still, it made him long for Budge's wonderful cooking. Oh well, soon, he hoped.

After eating, he left the café and headed for the livery stable to saddle his horse. Since there was no telegraph office in Contention, he needed to ride over to Tombstone to send a message to his employer to let him know he'd been unsuccessful in locating the boy and ask for further instructions.

Preacher was leading his Mustang outside when he heard a man call, "Rooney! Hey you! Ya kilt m' brother, and now I gotta kill you! So, get out here and face me. C'mon now. I'm waiting."

Preacher looked in the direction of the shouting and saw a man standing in the middle of the street, down near the Silver Dollar Saloon. He pushed his horse back inside the building to get him out of the line of fire and started walking toward the man in the street. It was too early in the morning and too nice a day for someone to have to die.

As he neared the man, Preacher could see that he was young. Not more than twenty, he thought. He was dressed in dusty, black denim pants with a black and white checked shirt and a tan buckskin vest. A Texas-style brimmed hat was pulled down low over his eyes. A single Colt was tied down on his right leg.

When Preacher was about twenty yards away, the youngster called, "That's far enough. Now draw!" The young man went into a kind of crouch with his left leg forward, right leg back, knees bent, and right hand hooked like a claw over the butt of his pistol.

Preacher kept walking at the same steady pace.

"I said that's far enough. Now fill your hand!" the youngster shouted again.

Preacher kept walking.

"Consarn you, stop!" the young gunman shouted.

Preacher kept walking. Now they were only about three feet apart.

The young gunman started to uncoil from his crouch, his knees began to straighten a bit, and he held out his left hand as if to ward Preacher off. "Dern you, back up so's I kin kill you proper!" he snarled.

But Preacher took one more step and his right hand shot out, fast as a striking rattler, grabbed the young man's nose, and twisted, hard! The man's hands shot to his offended snout as blood began to gush. Preacher dropped his hand to grab the man's gun from its holster and tossed it into a water trough.

Still holding his nose with his left hand, the young man dropped his right hand to paw at his empty holster. He bawled, "I'm gonna kill you!" But with all the blood running down his throat, it came out more as a gurgle.

Preacher grabbed the young man's shirt with his right fist and got quite a handful of chest hairs at the same time. He yanked the kid right up into his face and said quietly, "Your brother didn't give me a choice. But now *you've* got one. Go get your nose fixed and live to fight another day." With that, he pushed the man away and slapped him hard across the face with his left hand.

The youngster fell on his back in the dust, and Preacher turned and began to walk back to the stable.

But as he went, a crowd of eight or ten other young gunmen rushed out of the saloon, and one of them yelled, "Get im! Don't let him get away!"

Preacher abandoned his walk and broke into a sprint to the stable, jumped on his mustang, and rode out of town at a flat-out gallop.

As he went, he heard another voice holler, "Git yer horses. Git after him!"

With Dog pacing beside him, he lit a shuck for someplace else.

* * * * *

Preacher flew out of town, but as the last building fell away behind him, he slowed Jim to a walk and looked back over his shoulder to see if there were any signs of pursuit. A large cloud of dust arose back there. Those young toughs must have had their horses all saddled and ready, and they were going to be on his trail soon. He looked ahead and realized this track would lead him right past the farm of his new friend, Wayne Young. The last thing Preacher wanted to do was to bring trouble down on that good man.

He urged Jim to walk in a tight circle there on the road to leave tracks that would look like he was undecided as to which way to go, and then he left the trail and rode into the desert to the west. He kneed his mustang to a fast canter and chased his shadow past clumps of mesquite, sage, and prickly pear.

After about a mile, he turned in the saddle to make sure the young gunmen were still following. The cloud of dust was still there and seemed to be closing on him. Ahead was a range of low hills, and Preacher could see that there were several jumbles of huge boulders at the base of those hills. It looked like a good place to lose the men who were trailing him. He headed for those hills, riding easy in the saddle.

In a short time, he reached the boulders and began laying down a confusing trail in and out among the huge rocks, then up one of the hills and back down into the boulders again. Over and over he left confusing tracks that would take his pursuers a long time to figure out. That is, if they had a decent tracker among them. Otherwise, he would lose them completely, and that was not what he wanted. Not yet anyway.

He rode to the top of a low hill and found bedrock swept clean of dust or sand by the desert winds. He followed the bare stone for a way and then rode to the top of a second, taller hill, and there he dismounted. He led his mustang to a patch of dry, sparse buffalo grass and left him ground hitched there. He gave Dog a chunk of jerky from a saddle bag and taking his Winchester, went to a small gully in the side of the hill where he settled down to wait and see what his followers would do next.

* * * * *

The small gully Preacher was nestled in was as comfortable as a hammock. With the warm sun on his back, he slipped into a light doze. Much later he was roused by shouts from below. He eased his head above the rim of the gully and saw nine mounted riders circling among the boulders at the base of the first hill.

One of them followed his tracks up the lower hill and sat there looking around. His gaze went to the top of the taller hill where Preacher waited, and for a moment, that gaze lit on the spot where Preacher lay watching from his small gully. Preacher remained still and the gaze swept over him.

As the young man sat there studying the hillside, Preacher studied him. He wore blue denim trousers, a faded blue shirt, and black leather vest with a creased-crown hat. Dirty blond hair hung down over his collar, and his unlined face was shaved clean. All in all, a good-looking youth. Preacher kind of wondered what could have caused the man to choose the outlaw trail. Or maybe the outlaw trail had chosen him? It happened too often that a youngster in high spirits let circumstances get away from him and then found himself on the wrong side of the law.

Eventually, the youth spotted the tracks that led back down the hill and into the boulders. He reined his horse around to follow the tracks down the hill.

The nine mounted outlaws spent most of an hour trying to sort out the confused trail Preacher had left. Finally, they gathered together near the pile of boulders to confer. Some pointed off to the south, some west and over the range of hills, and others seemed to opt for heading back to Contention.

Ultimately, that group seemed to hold sway, and they all turned their horses, prepared to head back to where they came from. Preacher picked out that one youngster with the crease-crowned hat and drew a careful bead with his Winchester. When he pressed the trigger, that hat went flying like a kite in a hurricane. All nine hit the ground, running for the shelter of the rocks, pulling their six guns, and blasting away, even though they were way out of handgun range.

Preacher sent two more shots to splatter off the rocks just to keep their heads down before crawling back to his horse, tightening his cinch and riding over the back side of the hill and off to the west again. He did nothing to try to hide his trail.

Among the rocks, the young guns stayed hunkered down for nearly an hour before one raised his hat on a stick and got no answering fire from above. So, he raised his head a mite, ready to duck back down in an instant, but still no answering fire and they realized their quarry had left. It took them another hour to gather up their horses and for one of them to retrieve his bullet-riddled hat.

By the time they rode to the top of the hill, the sun was nearly touching the western horizon. But they decided to follow 'Bill Rooney's' tracks for as long as there was light to see.

CHAPTER EIGHT

Preacher rode a touch north of due west all day. He wanted to make sure he was nowhere near Fort Huachuca before he hatched his plans. When the sun was almost ready to touch the far horizon, he stopped to cut a leafy branch from a Palo Verde tree and, with a rope, drug it behind him as he changed his direction to due north. With a stiff breeze blowing across the desert, all trace of his passage was eliminated. Just before sundown, he found the tracks of a pair of wild burros.

Knowing a burro will not stray far from a water source, he followed the tracks into a nearby canyon where he found a seep of clear, cold water. The seep formed a small pool surrounded by lush, green grass. So, he unsaddled his mustang and prepared to make camp. Dog disappeared for a short time, only to return with a plump prairie dog dangling from his fearsome jaws.

Since Dog had provided his own dinner, Preacher poured a bit of sweetened oats from a sack in his saddle bags onto a flat rock to supplement the grass that Jim would eat. He then gathered some dry mesquite wood to make a small fire for coffee. The dry mesquite would burn hot and produce very little smoke. Not that he was concerned his pursuers might see his fire, just that he hated to get the campfire smell of woodsmoke on himself and his clothes.

When the coffee was ready, he poured himself a cup and dunked a hard, store-bought biscuit in it to soften it some. He finished his supper with a thick chunk of jerky. He then put out his fire, unrolled his blankets, and went to sleep.

* * * * *

Preacher awoke when the sun was just beginning to lighten the eastern sky. He climbed up the hill behind him to look the country over with his field glasses. A little more than a mile away, he spotted the faint glow from a dying campfire. He swapped his boots for a pair of Apache moccasins from his saddle bags and, calling Dog to his side, took off walking toward where he had seen the fire.

The nine men pursuing him had picketed their horses, built a huge fire, and posted a guard while they slept. The guard was sleeping as soundly as the others as Preacher crept up on their camp. Silently he cut all nine horses loose from the picket line and then motioned for Dog to come to him. When the horses spotted and smelled that huge beast, they all took off in a panic.

The noise of their leaving didn't awaken the young men who had been hunting Preacher, so he sent Dog to follow and harrie the horses so they wouldn't stop running too close to the camp. Satisfied, he hiked back to his own camp and saddled his horse for the ride back to Contention. He figured if he kept to a straight course, he could be there by mid-afternoon.

* * * * *

Back in Contention, the town was quiet, which made sense, as a goodly portion of the town's outlaw element was currently stranded out in the desert. Preacher took his time giving his horse a good rubdown with a stiff brush. He was ruffling Dog's ears when a grey-haired man stepped out of the sun's glare and into the shadowed stable.

He was dressed in buckskin shirt and trousers, boots, and a narrow-brimmed hat. He had a Remington revolver riding butt forward on his left hip and a wicked looking Bowie knife on his right hip. He wore a full beard and had a long nose that canted off to one side. When he opened his mouth to speak, Preacher saw that his top middle teeth were gone. That and the scars on his walnut sized knuckles spoke of a man used to settling disagreements physically.

"You're Rooney," the man said, but not as a question. "Boss wants to see you."

Preacher eyed the man closely and realized that even though he was older, this was not a man he wanted to have to tangle with. So, he simply said, "Lead the way," and followed the man outside and onto the boardwalk.

When they reached the Silver Dollar Saloon, the old man cut down the alley and to the back door, just like before. They went inside and up to the top floor where his guide stopped by the same door Preacher had used the last time he was there. He tipped his hat to his guide and went inside.

Once in the room, he found the same scene as the last time he was there. A table holding two coal oil lamps with reflectors, shining into the room and leaving the barely seen people behind the table in shadow. He sat in the chair in front of the table and waited.

He heard the same faint scratching noise followed by a faint tearing sound. He now realized it was the sound of someone writing on aper with a pen and then tearing that paper off a pad.

The male voice behind the lights said, "You told me William...uh, the man who sent you here had cholera. Is that right?"

"Yep, that's what he told me."

"You also said he was getting better. Is that right?"

"Yep. That's also what he told me."

"What medicine did he use?"

"I don't have any idea. We only communicated by telegraph."

There were more of those scratching noises, and then the voice behind the lamps said, "I want you to find out what medicine he used!"

As Preacher was about to respond, there came a sudden pounding on the door. The door flew open, and the bartender came rushing in.

"Boss! The doctor from the Fort is here!"

A female voice from behind the lamps said breathlessly, "Bring him here! Quickly!"

The doctor, who was obviously waiting outside the door, stepped into the room. A lovely, auburn-haired woman in a snug-fitting sky-blue dress reached forward to grab the doctor by his arm and dragged him behind the table with her.

"He's in here, doctor. Please help him."

The male voice from behind the lamps said, "Rooney, you may go, but stay close."

The bartender grabbed Preacher by the arm and pulled him out of the room. Preacher allowed himself to be pulled. The old man in buckskins was still waiting outside in the hall.

"C'mon downstairs, pardner. I'll buy you a beer," he said to Preacher.

* * * * *

Captain Ezekiel Dyer, the post surgeon from Fort Huachuca, spent a long time examining the young man lying on the sweat-soaked sheets in the back room.

Finally convinced that he really was looking at a case of cholera, he began mixing several powders in a glass of cold water. He lifted the young man's head and held the glass to his lips.

The young man took a sip, then shook his head and tried to push the glass away. "Sorry, son. I know it tastes bad, but you have to drink it. It'll do you good."

He put the glass back to the boy's lips and again he took a small sip, and then another. With the doctor's constant prodding, the glass was soon empty, and after a minute, the boy seemed to relax. His body stopped its thrashing and in another few minutes, he fell asleep.

The auburn-haired woman watched these proceedings and was amazed.

"That's a miracle!" she enthused. "What did you give him?"

"Oh, it was mostly bicarbonate of soda to calm his bowels and some morphine for pain plus a few other things. He should sleep for a while now. But the question is, who else has been in contact with him?" Doctor Dyer asked.

"Well, me, of course. I'm his mother. And some of the girls from downstairs, my secretary, and...let me think..."

Dyer said, "Well, you fill out that list, then get some beds in here. That main room is plenty big enough. Get some beds in here and then get everyone who has had contact with this boy into those beds. You might have a major infestation here. It has only been this boy's strong constitution that has kept him alive 'til now. Hurry and get those people away from the rest of the town folks before they all end up dead!"

"Dead!" she gasped. "Do you mean he's going to die? But he looks so much better now."

"That's because he's drugged. He's exhausted. Worn out. If we can control his symptoms and build up his strength some, he might make it. But others might not be so lucky, so get them up here. Now!"

CHAPTER NINE

Downstairs in the saloon, Preacher sat at a table with his buckskinned guide. The bartender sat two foamy mugs of beer in front of them. Preacher took a taste. Cold! Seems like everybody in this town had an icehouse.

He turned to his guide and said, "What's your name, sir? Seems like I've seen you somewhere before."

"Naw, you ain't' seen me, but you likely seen some of them I used to run with. I rode with Jim Bridger for a while. Fact is, he saved me one time when I ran afoul of a big ol' grizzly what woke up mean one day. Bridger shot that beast right through the head from a hundred and fifty yards. Kept me from getting et, but I'll carry the scars from that beast the rest of my days. Name's Hezekiah James."

Preacher looked hard at the old man. Yeah, take away the beard, straighten that nose, and sure enough, you'd be looking at Jesse. This must be a close relative, but in Contention, it's never a good idea to ask too many questions.

"Well, here's to you, Hezekiah. Glad that bear didn't finish the job."

Hezekiah raised his glass and said, "I'll drink to that, Preacher."

Preacher said, "Uh, the name is Rooney, sir."

"Sure it is! But don't worry, I ain't gonna shout it out, but I seen you a time or two as well. Know what you kin do with a six-gun, I do."

Preacher looked hard at the man for a bit, then relaxed. His secret was safe, he knew. He clinked his glass with Hezekiah's, and they both drained their beers.

As the two men continued to talk quietly, a shadow fell over them and the table where they sat. Looking up, Preacher first saw a man he didn't recognize but looking behind him saw a younger man whose nose was a swollen, purplish mass and both eyes were black. It was the young punk that had called him out earlier for the killing of his brother. Preacher was surprised at the amount of damage his nose twist had caused. Surprised, but not concerned. At least the kid was still alive. But apparently not finished with Preacher yet.

Preacher had to swivel around in his chair to see the outlaw who was standing directly behind him. That man was a brute. His massive shoulders topped a chest like a whiskey barrel. His arms were short but heavily muscled, ending in hands that looked like hammers. His legs were curiously small, given the size of the rest of the body.

He was wearing blue denim trousers stuffed into short boots and a gray shirt that strained to contain those huge shoulders and chest. A mat of curly black hair appeared at the open throat of that shirt.

The brute gently laid one of those massive hands on Preacher's shoulder and said with a voice that sounded like a growl, "You're the one what likes to beat up on young guys."

Preacher turned back to Hezekiah James to see the older man had his Remington in his hand, pointed in the direction of the brute behind Preacher. "Go ahead, Rooney. I'll make sure no one interferes in this here donnybrook."

Preacher shrugged off the hand on his shoulder and stood to face the man behind him. Rising to his full height, he found the brute only came up to his chin but still outweighed him by thirty or forty pounds.

"And what?" Preacher asked. "Are you the one who protects the little boys who like to play with guns?"

"Yep," the brute growled. "Name's Chancey, case you want to know who's about to put ya in the ground."

With that, Chancey swung a ham sized left fist at Preacher's midsection. That blow came without warning and had all the power of those huge shoulders behind it. The blow was obviously intended to put Preacher out of commission so Chancey could then take him apart at his leisure. Preacher was sure the tactic had worked well many times before, but Preacher was the survivor of too many knuckle-and-skull bouts to be taken in so easily. He simply took a quick half step back so that the blow sailed harmlessly past. Having missed his intended target, Chancey stumbled forward, off balance as he tried to get his feet under him again.

But Preacher didn't give him the opportunity. He swung with a left of his own that exploded on Chancey's mouth, pulping his lips and loosening several teeth. Preacher immediately followed that left with a right fist that buried itself in Chancey's belly, driving the breath from his lungs. Chancey doubled over with a gasp and took an involuntary step back that saved him catching another left that was aimed at his belly.

As Preacher set himself up for another blow, Chancey took another step back and looked at Preacher with a new level of respect. Usually in a bout like this, Chancey simply overwhelmed his opponent by sheer brute power. All he knew and understood was overpowering whoever he was facing. He knew nothing about boxing, but it seemed that this man did, and Chancey was facing a far different kind of opponent.

Having regained his breath, Chancey stepped forward, cocking his right fist, but at the last second swinging his left like a hammer that caught Preacher high in the ribs and nearly knocked him to the floor. If he went down, Chancey was prepared to jump on him with both feet and likely stomp him to death.

But Preacher was able to grab the back of a chair and keep himself from going down. He straightened himself and faced the shorter man with respect for the raw power in the man. That last blow may have cracked a rib. He fell back on the lessons he'd learned while sparring with a man who was a first-class boxer during lulls in the fighting in that miserable war.

He shot out a straight left into Chancey's face, opening a small cut below his right eye, and followed it with a left to the jaw and another right to the mouth, this time knocking out at least one tooth.

Chancey shook his head like an angry bull and swung his right fist overhand like a blacksmith throwing a hammer at a hot horseshoe.

The blow was too slow and too obvious. Preacher side-stepped away from it and stabbed a left into the big man's nose. He felt bones break and saw blood gush. Chancey went mad and began throwing overhand lefts and rights that had no specific targets, just hoping to hammer the man in front of him to the dirt.

Preacher stepped from side to side, avoiding every blow and jabbing his fists into the heavier man's face, seemingly at will. The barrage of blows was too much for the shorter man, and his knees collapsed before he fell face first to the barroom floor.

The kid whose nose Preacher had tweaked earlier, stood looking in amazement at his fallen champion, then turned and hurried out of the saloon.

Preacher untied the kerchief from around his neck and used it to wipe sweat from his face. He turned back to the table where Hezekiah was just sliding his Remington back into his holster.

"How about you coming with me? I know a place that's a lot quieter and the beer's just as cold."

Hezekiah rose and followed Preacher out the door.

CHAPTER TEN

With the arrival of the doctor from the military post, things began to change in Contention. Before he came, some of the working girls from the Silver Dollar Saloon had become ill. They 'had a bug.' But still they were required to work. And the townsmen who tarried with those working girls often caught that 'bug.' And as often as not, they took that 'bug' home with them and shared it with their wives who also became ill with the 'bug.'

But with the arrival of the doctor, that 'bug' suddenly had a name. And the name was cholera, a name that struck fear in the hearts of those who heard it. Business at the Silver Dollar fell off to next to nothing. There were a few devil-may-care types who laughed at those who retreated in fear and claimed they weren't worried about no 'bug.' But for most, that 'bug' represented a deadly threat. Anyone who showed those bright red fever spots on their cheeks was shunned, refused entrance into places of business, or even refused contact with good friends.

In the Cantina at the opposite end of the street, life went on as usual. The beer was still cold, the poker games were still friendly, and Preacher still spent several hours soaking his bruised knuckles in a bath of warm salt water. But most of the swelling was gone, and the few places where the skin was split had healed nicely. The details of the fight with Chancey were related to everyone who came into the place. The main difference was the poker game now had four players since Hezekiah James had become a regular.

Preacher had made his trip to the telegraph office in Tombstone to tell his employer what had transpired and then enjoyed a scalding hot bath at Sing Wan's laundry while he waited for a reply.

The reply came quickly. William Wells, Preacher's current employer, had responded by saying he was basically cured from his bout with cholera. The medicine that had helped the most was plain Bicarbonate of Soda, with liberal applications of morphine. And he further instructed Preacher that he was to do whatever was necessary to free his son and return him to his father as soon as possible.

On returning to Contention, Preacher had passed along to the doctor what he had learned about the medication his employer had used to overcome his bout with cholera.

The doctor was pleased but not surprised to hear that his original course of medication had been correct. That news was broadcast throughout the town to the extent that every package of Bicarbonate was sold out within hours. And some people were helped by it, but others, maybe those of weaker constitutions, were added to the town's cemetery.

* * * * *

Four days after nine young men had torn out of town in hot pursuit of one 'Bill Rooney', eight footsore young men staggered back into town. One of their number had succumbed to thirst on the long walk back. And the ones who'd survived had lost their appetite for chasing Rooney any further.

The cook, who had abandoned his job at the Longhorn Café for a better paying position at the Silver Dollar Saloon, had now taken up his final position six feet underground at the cemetery; while the blacksmith from the stable had recovered from his bout with cholera and was now back at work at his forge.

And out in the street in front of the Cantina, those same two young brothers were back and again tormenting something they had found with a pair of sticks. This time when Precher rose up to see what they were deviling, he saw a huge scorpion, its front claws waving in threatening arcs while poised high above its back, that venomous stinger was ready to deliver a killing strike. The two boys looked far too fascinated with their find to let the creature go.

But danged if history wasn't repeating itself, as one of those boys glanced down the street, then poked his brother so he'd look, too. Then both boys rose to their feet and disappeared down the alley. Preacher turned to see what had spooked the boys and here comes Chancey, walking down the center of the dusty street with the kid whose nose Preacher had tweaked walking right beside him.

They stopped right outside the Cantina, and Chancey called out, "Rooney, get out here! Gotta kill ya. So, c'mon out!"

Preacher stepped out onto the boardwalk. Hezekiah stood in the doorway, and Mickey and Pedro watched through the window.

Preacher spoke loudly, "Chancey, go home. We had our set-to, and now it's over. Just go home."

"Can't do that, Rooney. You're the onliest one ever whipped me with fists, and I respect that. But still, I gotta kill ya, so get out here."

Preacher looked over the unlikely pair, one tall and thin, the other short and squat. Both of Chancey's eyes were black, while the younger one's eyes had faded to a faint yellowish color. The kid's nose now had a permanent hump in it, and when Chancey opened his mouth to speak, he was missing two front teeth on top and one on the bottom.

They looked like they should have had enough, but they seemed bound to push for more. Preacher looked at them and didn't want to have to kill them. Chancey's arms were too short and muscular for him to make a fast draw, and the kid...well, he seemed content to let the brute do the fighting for him.

"Really, guys," Preacher said, pleading, "the fighting is over. Just go home!"

Chancey answered, "Can't do that, so get out here. I'm gonna count to three, and then I'm gonna shoot whether you're ready or not."

Reluctantly, Preacher stepped off the boardwalk to face the two in the street. Again, he said, "Really, guys, don't..."

But Chancey had already grabbed the butt of his Colt and was swinging it up to fire, a lot quicker than Preacher would have expected but still way too slow. Preacher drew his pistol and snapped a shot into the right elbow of the arm holding the gun. Preacher swore he heard the snap of the tendon that held the mighty bicep attached at the elbow. The bicep flew upwards to coil just below the shoulder.

Chancey grabbed at the injured muscle, but his arms were too short to reach. So instead, he dropped his left hand to grab for his pistol and sought to bring it back to bear on Preacher who was then forced to put a second round into that left elbow. Preacher didn't know what kind of life Chancey would have with both his strong arms ruined, but he would *have* a life.

While Preacher was still watching the man he had just crippled, he heard the kid sob, then cuss, and then saw out of the corner of his eye as the kid grabbed his own pistol and yanked it from the holster.

"Aw, c'mon, kid. My gun's already in my hand. Stop it!"

But the kid didn't stop. He continued to swing the pistol to bear on Preacher who snapped a third shot at the hand that held the Colt. He saw a piece of thumb go flying as the pistol was knocked into the air.

Then Preacher's gaze took in both men. He saw Chancey standing with his gun at his feet, both arms hanging down, and blood dripping off his fingers to form two small pools in the dust, and the kid holding his injured hand in his other hand as big tears coursed down his cheeks. He was looking at two men whose outlaw careers were now over. As he watched, the two looked at each other, and then turned and began the long slow walk back to the Silver Dollar Saloon.

Preacher watched them go, holstered his pistol, spat in the dust, and went back inside the Cantina.

He got back inside in time to see Mickey slap Pedro on the back and say, "Didn't I tell ya? Faster than Hickock, by golly!"

Hezekiah stepped away from the bar and pushed a fresh mug of cold beer into Preacher's hand, saying, "Here ya go, Pard. Drink up. I could tell ya didn't wanta do that, but sometimes they just won't let it go."

* * * * *

Later, Hezekiah watched as Preacher disassembled and cleaned his pistol with hot soapy water to remove every trace of black powder residue from the barrel. Then, he carefully oiled each piece, reassembled, and reloaded it. As he watched, he became curious.

"Mind if I ask you why you use that old-timey pistol 'stead of a newer Colt or Remington? Wouldn't a took you half the time to clean it."

Preacher answered, "Yeah, it would be more convenient. But the Colt weighs nearly two pounds more. Plus, mine has the tighter lands and grooves cut into the barrel for extra accuracy, and this barrel is almost two inches longer for greater range as well. But I guess mostly, I've just used this weapon for so long, without it, I'd feel like a part of myself was missing."

"Well, I reckon I can see that. I oncet had a Kentucky Rifle like that. Well, I'm gonna wander over to the Silver Dollar. It's payday, and the Boss owes me some money. See ya in a bit."

CHAPTER ELEVEN

In the evening, when Hezekiah James returned to the Cantina, he had a report to share with the others. "It's like a hospital over there. Most everybody's sick, even The Boss. But the kid's doing a bunch better. He's up and walking around. Weak as a kitten, but he's up."

"Hmmm. This might be the chance I need," Preacher said. "Maybe I should go over there and have a little look-see myself. I'll see you fellas later." With that, he rose and went outside.

Within a few minutes he was at the back door of the Silver Dollar Saloon. No one was in sight as he carefully opened the back door and stepped inside, pulling the door shut behind him. He stood there in the dark for a time, letting his eyes adjust to the dimness inside and listening carefully for any sound. All he heard was the sounds of distant coughing coming from up the stairs.

Silently, he mounted the staircase, and as he got closer to the top, the sounds of coughing and groaning got louder. He arrived at the door he'd twice been brought to. When he opened it, he found the room completely changed. The table and chair where he'd been interviewed were gone. In their place was at least a dozen iron bedframes, each one occupied. The room smelled strongly of human waste.

As he made his way to the smaller bedroom in the corner, he saw The Boss lying in one of the beds. He only knew it was her because of the mass of auburn hair, now soaked with sweat. Her eyes followed him, fever-bright and black as coal. He hurried past her and opened the door to the bedroom.

As he stepped inside, he saw the tow-haired young man seated on the side of the single bed.

"Are you James Wells?" Preacher asked.

"Yes. Who are you?"

"Doesn't matter. Your father sent me to bring you home. If you want to go, that is. How about it?"

"Oh, yes! Three men grabbed me while my father was so sick, and they dragged me here. I thought I was going to die here. But yes, I want to go home!"

"Alright. I'll go get some horses. I want you to meet me at the back door in fifteen minutes. Be at the backdoor by then; don't make me come up here and get you. Do you hear?"

"I hear, and I'll be there. I *have* to get away from these horrid people."

"Alright then," Preacher said. "Get moving. Fifteen minutes!"

He hurried out the way he'd come. The Boss's eyes followed him as he left.

* * * * *

Preacher threw saddles on Jim and a long-legged bay mare that had a deep chest and looked like she could travel. When he left the stable, he stopped at the Cantina to say goodbye to his new friends there. Hezekiah James said, "If you don't mind, I'd just as soon go with you. I've been here way too long, starting to get all citified and such."

"Fine with me," Preacher answered. "Glad to have you along. Meet me behind the Silver Dollar in five minutes."

With that, Preacher swung into his saddle and headed to meet the youngster he'd come here to rescue.

James Wells was terribly weak from his long illness, but he was sure he could ride alright. He started for the hallway, and as he passed the bed on which his mother lay, she clutched at him with a hand that had no strength. She tried to speak, but her fever-chapped lips just cracked and bled. While she tried to make the words come, he shook her hand off and said, "Why did you bring me to this nasty place, you vile woman?" And he hurried out of the room.

When he went out the back door, Preacher was there waiting and helped him into the saddle. As they were getting set, Hezekiah James rode up on a beautiful buckskin with black mane and tail.

"Glad you made it, Hezekiah. Let's get out of here." And off they went, racing down Main Street and north into the desert.

* * * * *

The three-quarter moon made the white desert floor almost as bright as midday as the trio rode away from the outlaw town of Contention. If they'd taken the time to look back, they'd have seen the bright gleam of flames erupting from the top floor of the Silver Dollar Saloon, caused by The Boss trying to get out of her bed to go after her son, where she knocked over a lantern and set the room afire.

* * * * *

Preacher and his companions rode north and a bit west until the moon had set and the sun was just beginning to lighten the eastern sky.

He rode up a broad canyon to a point where the canyon ended in a sheer granite cliff. The cliff was undercut at the bottom, providing enough room for the men and horses to stay in the shade as the sun rose on their right.

"This'll do for us to camp. We'll spend the hottest hours here and continue after the sun goes down. I don't know if we'll have anybody after us, but no use taking chances."

Hezekiah built a small fire and made coffee while Preacher picketed the horses and watered them from a bag he'd brought from the stables. The old frontiersman then volunteered to keep the first watch, so Preacher and the kid rolled out their blankets and went to sleep.

Much later, as the moon was again shedding its light on the desert floor, the trio of men were back in their saddles and riding into the Whetstone Mountains. There had been no sign of pursuit during the day, so they rode at a fast walk, sparing the horses. As dawn was approaching, Jim began to show signs of wanting to turn to the west.

Knowing the desert-bred mustang could smell water from a great way off, he called a halt. When the other two gathered beside him, he told them, "My horse is pretty sure there's water yonder, and we could use a refill for our canteens. I think we should let him follow his nose."

Hezekiah said, "Good idea. I once had a horse that could smell water like a birddog could smell quail. Let him have his head. We'll follow."

Preacher patted Jim on the neck and said, "Alright, boy, go get it." The mustang led them straight into the foothills of the Whetstones and then north along the sheer mountain walls.

They came to a spot where sand and small rocks had been piled into a mound with a sunken top. Then, around a corner, they came to a pool that someone had spent a lot of time enlarging. The pool was about the size of a bathtub and lined with tightly fitted rocks. Cold, clear water oozed from a vertical crack in the mountain wall to fill the pool, then ran out to disappear in the desert sand.

Beside the pool was a rough shelter made from mesquite poles and saguaro ribs. An ancient bedroll and a pile of rags were under the shelter. A name had been scratched into the rock wall that read, "Dead Mule Spring."

The three men let their horses have their fill at the pool while they filled everything they had with cool water.

As they were so engaged, the pile of rags under the shelter stirred, and a grizzled face began to appear. It was a thin face with skin drawn so tight it looked like the skull the skin was covering. A beak of a nose split the face and when the mouth opened, it revealed a few remaining teeth that were large and green. Washed out blue eyes regarded the three men silently for several seconds before a wheezing voice asked, "Y'all real?"

In an instant Preacher had wheeled and had his pistol pointed at the thing among the rags. "Who the heck are you?" he barked.

"Don't need no shootin' iron, mister. I'm...uh, I'm...Charlie. Mule Man Charlie is what they called me. This here is m' home."

Preacher holstered his weapon and walked over to where the old man waited, lying on the ancient bedroll.

"I'm Preacher. These here are Hezekiah and James. How long have you been here?"

"Uh, I don't rightly reco'member. I used to keep track o' the years by making a mark there," he said, pointing at a series of chiseled lines in the rock face. "But I fergot fer a spell. Don't rightly know. Y'all are the first persons I ever seen in all that time."

Preacher saw that there were at least a dozen lines cut into the stone. "You've been here all alone all this time?"

"Yep. I was prospecting 'round here when we ran outta water for three, four days, and it was powerful hot. Then Sal smelled water. Sal was my mule. My good ole mule, she was. I let her seek it, but she died, right over there," he said, pointing at the mound of sand and rocks.

"I buried her right where she fell, and then found this here spring. If she coulda held on jest a couple more minutes, we'd a been alright. She'd still be alive." As he said this, a big tear rolled down his grizzled old cheek. "Loved that mule, I did."

He was quiet for a few minutes. Then he continued, "I built this here house," he said, indicating the shelter where he laid. "An' even found some gold right here. Mined it for a while, hoping somebody'd come along and hep me get back to Benson, but y'all are the first humans I seed in all that time. Got old, I did, and mine petered out. But I got, must be twenty sacks of high-grade gold ore stacked right under this here blanket." He patted where he was lying.

By now, Hezekiah and young James had joined Preacher under the shelter. He recapped what the old man had told him, then asked Charlie, "What do you live on? Where do you get food?"

Charlie said, "Jack rabbits mostly. Sheep once in a while. Mountain sheep. Got me an old steer one time. Danged old thing was tougher than I was. But I smoke 'em, and it lasts me a while. Ain't had nothin' in 'bout a week now, though."

Without another word, the three men began putting together a meal. They built up a fire in the firepit Charlie had created and set coffee on to boil. When the old man smelled that, he broke out in tears again.

"Lordy, but don't that smell good? I ain't smelled coffee cooking in years. Used to love it, I did."

Young James quickly poured a cup and handed it to the old man. He brought the scalding brew to his cracked old lips and gulped a huge swallow down. "Oh, lordy, but ain't that good?" he repeated. James took the cup from him, had to pull it away from the old man, to refill it and hand it back. Charlie accepted it gratefully and this time sipped it much slower, savoring every sip.

Hezekiah had killed a sage hen with a rock as they rode across the desert last night and had plucked it while they rode. Now he spitted it over the fire. While it cooked, he mixed up a batch of frying pan biscuits. When all was ready, he divided the meal four ways, and old Charlie again was moved to tears as he ate.

"Oh, lordy, but you guys put on a feed." Young James was kept busy refilling the old man's coffee cup.

When the meal was finished and the three newcomers had cleaned up, Old Mule Man Charlie rolled himself back up in his ratty old blankets and went off to sleep, a smile on his wizened old face.

CHAPTER TWELVE

When the new day began to brighten the rocks, Preacher awoke to find the old man was gone. He quickly shook out his boots, slipped them on, and went hunting for him. He wasn't at the spring or the old mine. But when Preacher stepped around the corner of the cliff, he saw the old man seated on the mound where Charlie had told them he had buried his mule. Preacher approached quietly and saw the old man's eyes were wet with tears.

The old man looked up when Preacher approached, and Preacher said, "Good morning, Charlie. Are you alright?"

"Oh, sure. Sure, right as rain. I used to come out here every day just to sit with Old Sal. Loved that mule, I surely did. Never had no kin folks, so she was the onliest family I ever had. But then fer the longest time, I hadn't the strength to get here. But that good feed you put on yes'tidy, that perked me up real good, it did. Or maybe it was the coffee. I sure do thank ya fer it."

"Well, Hezekiah's got coffee made and is cooking up some bacon and beans for breakfast. Want me to bring you a cup?"

"Oh, I surely would 'preciate that, I would. I jist wanta sit here for a bit and visit with Sal. I ain't been able to get here fer a long while."

Preacher went to fetch two cups of coffee, one for each of them. When he got back, the old man was still sitting on the mound with his gnarled old hands on his knees and his head hanging down on his chest.

Preacher offered the cup, saying, "Here's your coffee, Charlie. Hezekiah says he'll have breakfast ready in five minutes."

The old man didn't move. Preacher spoke louder. "Here's your coffee, Charlie." But there was still no response from the old man. Preacher nudged one of Charlie's hands, but it just slipped off his knee and plopped down on the mound. He gently lifted the old man's head. His eyes were closed, and there was a faint smile on his lips. The old man and his mule were together again.

* * * * *

Preacher and Hezekiah worked together to dig the grave, and they buried Old Mule Man Charlie right close to the mound where Charlie had buried his mule,

Sal. They figured he'd want to lie next to her. Then they returned to his crude shelter.

As they were packing up and breaking camp, Hezekiah asked, "What are we going to do about Charlie's gold? I looked at one of the bags, and it's more than high grade. It's mostly gold, only a little quartz."

"I don't know," Preacher answered. "Last thing Charlie told me was that he had no kin. We could just leave it here, but that don't seem right either. Do you want it?"

Hezekiah scratched at one whiskery cheek before saying, "Well...I always did hanker after a little ranch of my own, up Wyoming way. Maybe quit wandering and run a few cows. Never could afford it, though. As much gold as is under that blanket would not only last me, but any grandkids I might have. Don't you want any of it?"

"No. I've already got me a real nice place and a little cash set by. Besides, I gotta get this kid back to his dad, and gold would just slow me down."

"Well, if you're sure, then I'll go back to Contention and get a couple pack horses, or mules if I can find them. And if you ever get up Wyoming way, look me up at Mule Man Ranch."

"You've got a deal, and good luck to you."

They all mounted up and left. Preacher and the kid went north, and Hezekiah turned and went back south.

* * * * *

When Hezekiah got back to Contention, he was amazed to see the top floor of the Silver Dollar Saloon was mostly burned off. They had been able to put the fire out before it spread to the rest of the building, but the loss of life had been great.

The only good news was that the fire seemed to have stopped the spread of cholera. There were no new cases anywhere in the town.

Hezekiah tied up outside and went into the saloon. As soon as he entered, three of the young toughs that had trailed Preacher out of town earlier jumped him, wrestled him into a chair and tied him to it. When he was secure, a horrible looking creature limped up to him and struck him across the face. He had to look several times before he recognized The Boss. Her mass of auburn hair was mostly burned away and her cheeks were black with burned skin. The hand that slapped him was blistered and black as well.

When she spoke, her voice was little more than a rasp. "Where did you take my son?"

Hezekiah realized that maybe hooking up with Preacher hadn't been such a good idea. He was thinking rapidly, trying to find a way out of this mess. "Pr... uh... Rooney! I saw that Rooney with some young fella. They was lightin' a shuck fer Tombstone, couple nights ago. I... uh... I didn't know he was stealin' your kid, though. Just saw 'em running. Had I knowed, I'd sure 'nough stopped him. For sure, I woulda, Boss!"

The Boss turned to the young outlaws who had tied him up and rasped, "Put him in the storeroom. Keep him tied and take some more men to Tombstone. Bring me back my son!"

Four of the outlaws carried Hezekiah, still bound to the chair, and shoved him in the storeroom and shut the door, leaving him there in the dark. They had tied his hands together and took several wraps of the rope around his chest and upper arms, securing him to the chair. They didn't take his gun or knife, but those would do him no good, as he couldn't reach them.

But on a thin cord around his neck and under his shirt, he wore a small Sioux arrowhead. He'd worn it there ever since he had cut it out of his leg, years back. If he could reach it, it was razor sharp and would easily cut the ropes that bound him.

The rough ropes binding him scraped and cut into the skin of his wrists as he twisted his hands against the ropes to get a couple fingers free. But eventually, he was able to get those fingers on the arrowhead. He abraded his wrists even more as he tried to twist his hands to a point where he could saw at the ropes that bound his hands together. But, when he was able, the ropes parted easily from the sharp little blade. In no time, he had cut himself loose and slipped out the back door.

Hezekiah made his way behind the buildings and down to the stable where the blacksmith knew nothing about his being tied up. But the stable man did have two mules that were broke to pack saddles, and for fifteen dollars each, he was happy to see them go.

Hezekiah made his way back up the single street, walking between the mules and holding onto their rope halters until he got to his horse. Swinging into the saddle and with a tug on the two ropes, he raced out of town, heading south.

When Preacher had fled from the young outlaws, he had taken care to leave a plain trail to follow. But Hezekiah, a veteran of many scrapes with Indians, wasn't about to leave a trail that could be followed, not once he was far enough out of town so they'd know which way he went. Before he got to the farm of Wayne Young, he left the trail, rode into the desert, and disappeared. As soon as he picked up Mule Man Charlie's gold, he was bound for Wyoming and the peaceful life!

CHAPTER THIRTEEN

Preacher and young James Wells, the lad he had been sent to bring back to his father after he had been snatched away by his mother, who just happened to be The Boss of a town filled with outlaws, rode slowly north through the desert after their hurried escape from Contention and the boy's mother. Preacher found that the boy's stamina had been severely sapped by the long illness he had suffered through. It was necessary to stop and rest often.

Preacher figured he was about one hundred miles from his home in Tucson. Ordinarily that would be an easy two-day ride. But he was going to have to consider the boy's weakened condition. It would take maybe four days of easy travel. He was concerned with delivering the boy to his father in good shape.

They settled into a plan of stopping about every hour so James could dismount and walk around a bit or lie down if shade could be found. When they traveled, Preacher kept the horses at a walk, which made Jim uneasy. Mustang born, he was eager for the trail and finding what was over the next hill. He wasn't happy with the slow pace, but loved and trusted Preacher enough to know that this was what he wanted, so this was what they'd do. As they traveled, Preacher kept a constant watch over their back trail, searching for the rising dust that would signal approaching riders. But he saw nothing.

What he should have done was pay more attention to where they were going than to where they had already been, because when trouble arose, they rode right into it.

It was going on midafternoon, and Preacher was looking for a place to stop so James could rest. As they crested a small hill, a beautiful valley opened up before them. A small stream entered the valley from the northeast and meandered across the lush meadow. As he thought about the unexpected greenness, he decided this must be a branch of the tail end of the San Pedro River. He hadn't expected to find anything like this so far south, but he welcomed it.

As the horses started down the hill and into the valley, Preacher turned once more in the saddle to check their back trail. When he turned back forward, an Indian was standing in front of him, holding an old Sharps side-hammer rifle across his chest. Preacher was startled by the man's sudden appearance.

The man was about five and a half feet tall with long black hair going gray at the temples. His hair was held back by a red bandana, and he wore knee-high moccasins, a long breech clout and a faded blue shirt with no buttons. His skin was the color of mahogany, and his black eyes regarded Preacher without blinking.

Aside from his sudden appearance, there was nothing threatening about him. Neither was there any welcome. He simply stood there, barring their way into the valley. Beadwork on the man's belt knife sheath led Preacher to believe the man was one of the White Mountain Apaches.

Recovering quickly from the man's sudden appearance, Preacher lifted his right hand and said, "Hough."

The Apache didn't respond to the greeting but stepped up beside Preacher's horse and reached to take the pistol from his holster. Preacher reached out and grabbed the man by the wrist and clamped down hard. The man blinked and glanced quickly at the hand that held his wrist in such a crushing grip.

Preacher released his grip, and the man's hand dropped to his side. The Indian then took a single step to the side and with a brief nod of his head, indicated that the two horsemen should precede him into the valley. Preacher nudged Jim with his knees and walked forward into the valley. As they dropped below the top of the hill, an encampment became visible.

There were five tipis pitched by the side of the stream and two crude shelters made of sticks and grass. Bachelor quarters, Preacher thought. He rode up to the camp and sat there on his horse, young James at his side looking scared to death.

CHAPTER FOURTEEN

When Preacher pulled up before the small encampment, an Indian, tall for his race and with long gray hair also held back by a red bandana, stepped out of the center tipi. He was dressed in much the same way as the Indian who had stopped them at the edge of the meadow, except his shirt was green and dirt stained. His face was deeply creased, and he had a nose as large and hooked as an eagle's beak.

Out of the various shelters stepped eight more warriors, five women, and several children who hid behind the legs of the adults while peeking out at the mounted white men.

Again, Preacher raised his right hand and extended the greeting, "Hough." The gray-haired Indian didn't' return the greeting but stared at the intruders with eyes as black and sharp as chips of flint.

After several minutes of silent appraisal between the two groups, Preacher said in English, "Has the mighty Taza nothing to say?"

This startled the old Apache who said, "You know me?"

Preacher was relieved that he had guessed correctly and answered, "Who does not know the eldest son of the mighty warrior, Cochise?"

Obviously pleased at being recognized, the old chief said, "And who are you, White Eyes?"

"I am called Preacher. This is my friend, James."

"Huh!" Taza grunted. "Then I also have heard of you, man-hunter. Why have you come here? Do you mean to force me to return to the white man's reservation? There are not nearly enough of you to do that!"

"No, mighty Chief. I seek only to return this young man to his father. I have no interest in trying to force so great a warrior as you to do anything that would cause your spirit to rebel. We are just passing through."

"Hmmm. Well said, man-hunter." He swept his left hand to indicate the meadow and continued, "You may go."

As preacher began to rein his horse around, the largest of the eight warriors shouted, "No!"

All eyes turned to this man as he stepped forward out of the group behind Taza. Most of the warriors were lean, slender men with long, wiry muscles. They stood about five and a half feet tall. But this man was nearly six feet tall with a broad chest and massive biceps. There was in his face a hint of the white man who had been his father thirty some years ago.

Taza turned to face the man and said, "Tall Elk, why did you speak?"

Tall Elk spoke roughly, "If you allow the man-hunter to go, he will tell the blue coats where we are. He will bring them down on us. He must not be allowed to go!"

"You would challenge your Chief, Tall Elk? I have already given my permission for these two to go in peace. Man-hunter is said to be an honorable man."

"Waugh! No white eyes is honorable! I challenge man-hunter to a trial by combat!"

"Hm. That is your right," Taza said. "Very well. Trial by combat it shall be!"

Tall Elk stepped forward and pulled a wicked looking Bowie knife from a sheath and stood in front of Preacher. Preacher kneed his mustang backwards several steps, pulling young James's horse with him. He undid his gun belt and handed it to James, saying, "If this goes badly, kill the big one first!"

He stepped down from his horse with his belt knife in his hand and cautioned Dog to remain still. Preacher's knife, with a five-inch blade, looked puny compared to the twelve-inch razor sharp blade Tall Elk held.

The Indians spread out to form a large circle with the two combatants in the center.

As Preacher approached Tall Elk, the Indian dropped into a crouch and swung his shining blade in a vicious arc designed to gut the man in front of him.

Preacher went up on his toes and arched his body so that the Indian's blade sailed harmlessly past. He swung his own, smaller knife down in a short arc that nicked the big man's shoulder.

Tall Elk backed up, surprised. He had engaged in many such contests with other men, both Indian and white. And while his body bore a few scars, he had come to believe that white men knew little about fighting with knives. But maybe this one was different. Maybe he had best be very careful. He began to circle to his right, keeping his wicked blade in front of him and watching to see if the white man would stumble.

But Preacher moved gracefully, light on his feet, and allowed Tall Elk to move around as he liked. His eyes watched the Indian like a rattle snake watches a pack rat. The Indian feinted with forward jabs several times, always falling back at the last second, trying to draw Preacher into following. But Preacher just kept watching, his own knife at the ready.

Finally, in a lightning move, the Indian switched his knife to his left hand and struck at Preacher's exposed right side. But Preacher saw the move coming and struck down with his blade, opening a long gash on the Indian's forearm.

Again, the Indian jumped back and switched hands, driving forward off his right foot and seeking to bury his blade in Preacher's chest.

Preacher reacted faster than Tall Elk thought possible and caught the Indian's blade with the guard of his own knife, pushed the Bowie away to his right and swung his hard left fist into the Indian's mouth, splitting his lips and knocking out two front teeth. The force of that blow knocked the big Indian to the ground, but he bounced to his feet before Preacher could move in and take advantage of the slip.

Now Tall Elk was bleeding from both arms and blood was dripping down his chest from his smashed lips. The Indian's confidence was now gone, and he was wishing he hadn't so foolishly challenged a man whose abilities he didn't know. He was now thinking he could very well lose this fight, and his spirit rebelled within him at the thought of being bested and killed by a hated white man.

As he jumped to his feet, his left hand grabbed a fistful of dust and flung it into Preacher's eyes. But again, Preacher saw the move coming and quickly shut his eyes and took a step toward Tall Elk, catching him with his left arm across his body. He swung his right fist, with the added weight of the hunting knife in it, into the Indian's jaw knocking him to the ground again. This time Preacher followed the big Indian down, placed his knee on the Indian's knife arm, and his own blade at Tall Elk's neck.

Tall Elk looked into the face of the white man with amazement. He was bested, and he saw his own death in the white man's eyes. He immediately began to sing his death song.

But Preacher wrested Tall Elk's knife from his hand and gave it a heave before rising to his feet and sheathing his own blade.

Tall Elk remained on the ground, staring at the white man standing over him. He couldn't understand that he was being offered mercy, which he certainly would not have given. But instead of mercy, he felt shamed!

The white man who was standing over him wasn't even breathing hard. Tall Elk rolled over, got to his hands and knees, and rose to his feet.

Without a backward glance, he fled in shame from his tribe. He may never be able to return.

Preacher walked to where young James sat on his horse, retrieved his gun belt, and strapped it on before turning back to Taza.

"Do we still have your permission to leave in peace?"

Without a word, the old Chief swept his left hand toward the meadow. Preacher got on his horse and led young James toward the far side of the small river. As he rode, he tried hard to control the shaking of his body that was setting in as the reality of their escape flooded through him.

* * * * *

After Preacher and James had crossed the small river, they stopped on the far bank to empty their canteens and water bags before refilling them with the fresh, cold water. As they worked, hate-filled eyes watched from the screening willows just upstream. Long after they had mounted up and left, those glaring eyes followed their progress until they were out of sight.

Tall Elk remained hidden until long after darkness had fallen and all sounds from the encampment had ceased. Then he crept, as silent as a shadow, to retrieve his knife. He then rose to his full height and left the meadow, running along the track that Preacher had taken. He would make this white man pay for humiliating him.

CHAPTER FIFTEEN

When Preacher and James Wells had traveled about twelve miles, they came to the foothills of the Rincon Mountains and a place where outlaws were known to gather. There was a cave there that was colossal in its extent. Bandits had long used the place as a hideout, but fortunately there was no one there when they arrived.

There was plenty of firewood laid up and a brush corral for the horses, so Preacher lit a fire and began cooking up some supper for James and himself. He was beginning to relax and look forward to putting an end to this long and dangerous task he had undertaken. His own bed and Budge's cooking was sounding better and better.

After eating, they rolled out their blankets and drifted into deep slumber.

* * * * *

The two white men had done nothing to hide their trail, so Tall Elk had no trouble following them. He had drunk deeply before crossing the river, back where Taza and his small band was camped, but had not had any water since then. Apache warriors were known to be able to travel farther with little or no supplies than any white man. And Tall Elk's ability to do without was great. But he was still the offspring of an Apache mother and a white father. Compared to a pure Apache, Tall Elk was suffering when he finally got to the place where Preacher and James were camped.

He sank down behind a large boulder and sat quietly until his sides quit heaving from the strain of his long run. But his thirst was maddening. Sitting quietly and watching the white men sleep was pure torture to him. Knowing the water his abused body demanded was just a few paces away, he had to fight his every instinct to rush into the camp and grab the water. He could almost feel the cool sweetness as it poured down his dry throat. His need for water was now even stronger than his need for revenge.

Finally, he could stand it no more. He rose to his feet and turned his back on the sleeping men. He forced himself to walk away from them and went back to the desert floor. By the light of the quarter moon, he sought for what he *had* to have. A mile from where Preacher was camped, Tall Elk finally spotted the leaning shape of a barrel cactus.

With a slash from his long knife, he slit the top off the cactus and buried both hands in the pulp inside. He pushed a handful of that pulp into his mouth and sucked at the moisture it contained. He'd been forced to find moisture this way in the past, and he remembered the awful taste the pulp left in his mouth.

But right now, with his thirst raging, he didn't even notice the moldy taste. He spat the pulp from his mouth and grabbed another handful. He had dug nearly to the bottom of the cactus before his thirst was slaked.

His screaming thirst finally satisfied, Tall Elk sat back on his heels and stretched his long arms out in gratitude to the sliver of moon that was riding low on the horizon. Then he lay back on the sandy desert floor and fell into a deep, exhausted sleep.

When he awoke, the sun had already cleared the distant mountain. He scrambled to his feet and jogged back to where Preacher had camped. The spot was empty. The men and horses were gone.

* * * * *

Preacher had long since abandoned any thought of outlaws from Contention following them. He didn't give *any* thought to the huge Indian that had tried to kill him. His thoughts were fixed on getting back home and finished with this retrieval task. Besides all that, he was coming to like this young man he was rescuing. James Wells was a polite and knowledgeable young man. Knowledgeable in the way of book learning, that is. He knew nothing about survival in a hostile atmosphere.

Still, he didn't complain about the harshness of the journey, even though it was obvious he was still suffering from the after-effects of his long illness.

To accommodate James's weakened condition, Preacher kept the horses at a walk, even though home was now so near. They'd get there soon enough. And he let himself relax. That could be a deadly mistake.

* * * * *

Tall Elk had been refreshed by the moisture the cactus had provided and by his sleep on the desert floor. But he'd had no food since the morning before, so his body hadn't completely returned to full strength. He jogged along, following the clear tracks of the two horses and one large dog.

He crested a small rise and saw the dust from the horses he was following. Through that dust, he could barely make out the dark form of the man who had shamed him.

Looking ahead, he could see the trail the riders were following made a large swing to the west to avoid a jagged jumble of rocks. Then it swung back north and through a very narrow pass between steep and rugged cliffs.

If Tall Elk could get to the pass before the riders, he could ambush and kill his enemy easily. He studied the jagged rocks this trail swung away from and thought he might be able to make his way through those rocks and get to the pass ahead of the hated white eyes.

Tall Elk didn't hesitate. He flung his already weakened body at the rocks and raced headlong to get ahead of Preacher and James Wells.

As he ran among the jumbled rocks, he was pleased to see they weren't as closely packed as they appeared from a distance. In fact, weaving in and out among them was fairly easy. He was certain he could get ahead of his enemies. He ran on.

As Preacher led James around the jumble of rocks, he felt a prickling of uneasiness, as if he were overlooking something obvious. He stopped and turned in the saddle to closely examine their back-trail. Nothing moved back there but a single roadrunner with a small lizard struggling in its beak.

He turned his sights ahead and examined the narrow pass they would soon have to travel. It made an excellent ambush point, but he couldn't imagine who or what might lie in wait for them. Still, he made certain to caution himself to take extra care ahead and to keep a sharp lookout behind as well. Usually when his senses made him aware of a possible threat, there was a good reason for it. He kneed Jim ahead, and James followed along.

* * * * *

Racing flat out through the scattered rocks, Tall Elk arrived at the pass well ahead of Preacher and James. Carefully searching the cliff side, he spotted a small cleft on the west side of the pass. There, he could crouch unseen until his enemy was right beside him. The cleft was about six feet up the side of the cliff, so he could leap out right at the white man's head. He scrambled up the cliff face and into the cleft. With his long knife in his hand, he was ready to vanquish his hated enemy. Maybe if he returned with the two scalps, he'd be welcomed back into the tribe.

CHAPTER SIXTEEN

Tall Elk's sides were heaving from his hurried race to get to this ambush place ahead of his enemy. His lungs craved oxygen and his thirst was returning. His lack of food was denying his body the fuel it needed, and the blazing sun, just shy of midday, was shining blindingly into his eyes. Just for a moment, he allowed his eyes to drift shut.

It seemed like a moment, but when he snapped awake and peeked down the trail to see how far away his enemy was, he found the lonely trail empty.

He almost jumped to his feet, thus revealing himself, but at the last moment stopped himself. Instead, he peeked to the north to find that the two men had nearly cleared the pass. They were almost a hundred yards ahead of him. Somehow, he had missed his chance to ambush them. Should he reveal himself now he would almost certainly be killed. How could he have allowed this to happen?

* * * * *

As Preacher and James cleared the dangerous pass and the broad, empty desert spread out before them, he paused and turned again to check his back trail. Had Tall Elk jumped out of his place of concealment at that moment, he would have been killed. But he stayed concealed in his cleft in the rock and, satisfied, Preacher urged his mustang on ahead.

Tall Elk watched until his enemy was several hundred yards ahead before easing his long body out of its place of concealment and sliding down to the trail. He had missed his chance to kill the enemy.

The big Indian stood in the middle of the pass and watched his enemy disappear into the distance. Now, in addition to his hunger and thirst, and the exhaustion that was gripping his body, he felt a new emotion. Self-loathing. He had always taken great pride in the fact that he was the largest warrior in his tribe, the strongest, and, in his mind, the smartest.

But now he had been humiliated by a smaller white man; he had let his body fall asleep when he should have been preparing to attack. And he was standing helplessly watching that enemy ride safely away.

No! He would not allow the enemy to escape his wrath so easily. Without another thought, he turned his weakened body in the direction where Preacher was disappearing and forced his tired body to run.

But he couldn't hold to the rapid pace he started with, and he began to slow until he hit an easy lope that was all he could maintain. If Preacher looked back now, he would surely see Tall Elk trailing after him. But he didn't. Home was too close for him to be concerned about what was behind him.

* * * * *

The sun was just sinking behind the Tucson Mountains as Preacher and James Wells rode into Tucson. The few wispy clouds that hung above those mountains turned to brilliant crimson and gold before darkness overtook them. Preacher rode to the stables, stripped the tack from the horses, gave both animals a good rubdown with a stiff brush, and poured a bit of the sweet feed that Jim loved for both horses before heading for the railroad station. There, they ascertained there was an eastbound train leaving the station at eight in the morning.

He led James to The Occidental Hotel where they ate in the saloon and went upstairs to bed.

Much later, a furtive figure crept into the city, being careful to remain hidden. Tall Elk had followed his enemy here, to this huge gathering place of whites. He had finally slaked his thirst from the muddy water of the Santa Cruz River. Now he slunk into the stable and assured himself the gray mustang he had followed so far was indeed there, as was the huge, ugly dog. Now he followed his nose to that barrel filled with molasses sweetened oats. He scooped the sweet feed into his mouth, crunching loudly on the oats and enjoying the sweetness of the molasses.

Then, silent as a shadow, he climbed into the hay loft where he burrowed deeply into the hay and gave in to his exhaustion. Tall Elk slept and dreamed of what he would do to his enemy on the morrow.

* * * * *

Come morning, Preacher rose and scrubbed his body as well as he could from the basin of water in his room. He then dug his last set of clean garments from his saddle bags and went to roust young James from his bed. They went down to the café and ate heartily after so many days of campfire cooking.

Before heading for the railroad station, Preacher took James to the clothing store where he outfitted him with decent traveling clothes. Preacher then added the cost of those clothes to his list of expenses and gave James the list to deliver to his father. He put the boy on the train bound eventually for New Orleans. He then sat down on a bench by the tracks and watched the train pull slowly away from town.

When the whistle faded away, he went back to the stable to retrieve the horses. As he stepped into the saddle, his faithful mustang knew where they were and where they were going. After such a long slow walk, Jim was eager to run, so Preacher let him have his head. They ate up the miles to home in short order.

Tall Elk slept the sleep of those who were completely used up. The food he'd eaten the night before went a long way toward restoring his great strength, but it was going to take many days before that strength was completely restored. When he finally dug his way out of the hay where he had slept, he heard the noises that white men make when they are busy doing things. He recognized the voice of his enemy as he talked to his horse.

When Preacher mounted up and rode away, the big Indian hurried down from the loft and peered through a crack in the board wall of the stable to see what direction he took.

Preacher rode due north toward the Santa Catalina Mountains, a route that took him through the center of town. Now what was Tall Elk going to do? He couldn't' very well follow him through so many of the white-eye enemies.

Tall Elk had to figure that Preacher wasn't going to stay in Tucson. And though Tucson was a large town by frontier standards, it wasn't all *that* big!

He retreated to where he'd come into town the night before, first filling a gunny sack with some of that sweet feed he'd eaten last night. He returned to the river he'd crossed the night before where there was plenty of brush to conceal him. Then he set out to walk around the city, hoping to be able to pick up the clear track of the mustang he had followed for so far.

* * * * *

If you were to set out to circumnavigate the city of Tucson, starting from the south, you would eventually come to River Road. River Road runs basically east and west but with more curves and dips than a sidewinder's tracks. It runs up hill and down, around obstacles, and through gullies and ravines but leads basically east and west.

Tall Elk found River Road and surmised that his quarry, traveling north, would have to at least cross this road. He jogged along, bent at the waist, and hunting by the light of the waning moon for the small hoofprint of the mustang and the huge paw print of the ugly dog.

When he found the tracks, he was surprised to see they turned to follow the road deeper into the foothills. He followed them.

CHAPTER SEVENTEEN

Few things look better than one's own home after a long absence. Preacher's snug stone cabin looked that way to Preacher when he finally rode into the yard. He dismounted and led his mustang into the stable where Dog immediately went to his favorite spot and laid down to sleep. As he was unsaddling his horse and rubbing him down, Budge came around the corner from his own apartment to greet his friend after the long journey.

"Howdy, Preacher. Good to see you! Guess you made it back alright? No problems?"

"Howdy, Budge. Nothing *but* problems! I gotta be more careful about the jobs I take. But it's good to be home."

"Well, there's coffee ready at the ramada. Come on out when you're ready, and I'll rustle up some grub."

"Thanks, Budge. You have no idea how good that sounds. I'll be right along."

Soon, the two old friends were seated at the table under the saguaro-rib roofed ramada, and Preacher was relating the events of his latest adventure.

Later, as the setting sun cast long shadows across the small canyon, they banked the fire and went to their separate homes to sleep. Preacher was looking forward to finally sleeping in his own bed.

Later still, as myriad stars wheeled overhead, a malevolent figure made his cautious way to the stable to see if a certain mustang was there. But as he got close, a deep, rumbling growl from Dog told Tall Elk that he was in the right place. He quickly turned and fled back the way he had come.

He climbed the canyon walls to get above the trim little homestead and secreted himself among some stunted Pinyon pines. From there, he would watch below and plot his revenge.

* * * * *

With the morning sun, Tall Elk was seated cross legged behind the screening branches of a stunted Pinyon pine and cutting the long tops off his moccasins. His long journey trailing the white eyed devil had worn the soles out of his moccasins, and he was forced to use the tops of his tall footwear to repair the bottoms.

As the white men began stirring around, the smell of brewing coffee set his mouth to watering. He had been fortunate enough to sample the white man's coffee several times and had come to love the taste. He especially liked the way the liquid made him feel energized and ready for anything! He licked his dry lips as the smells from below set his belly to rumbling. All he had left was a small handful of the sweet feed he'd stolen from the stable in Tucson. He began eating it, just one grain at a time, crunching carefully to make it last.

His hate for the white man grew.

* * * * *

Preacher slept late and woke slowly. For a minute, he lay quietly, just luxuriating in the feeling of 'home'. Finally, he climbed out of bed, grabbed a towel and a bar of soap, and headed for the creek for a good scrubbing. It had been way too long since his last bath.

Later, bathed and dressed, he accepted a cup of rich, hot coffee from Budge and watched as Dog, his huge Wolf Hound, prowled the yard with his nose in the air, trying to isolate one particular scent. Breezes in the canyon often swirled in strange patterns, deflecting off the canyon walls and swirling around the trees above before falling again into the canyon. Just now, there was something that Dog hated on that breeze, but he couldn't' pick it out. A low rumbling growl rose in his throat as he tried to sort out that scent.

When a moment of brief calm came, Dog stopped his prowling, stared at a spot atop the cliff behind the cabin, and turned to race out of the yard, headed for the top of the canyon.

* * * * *

Tall Elk had also slept late that morning. The sand where he lay still held some of the heat from the day, and he was exhausted from the long trail he had walked following the tracks of the white man who had so humiliated him.

When he was fully awake, he crept close to the cliff's edge to see what was happening in the homesite below. But when his face appeared at the top of the cliff, he found that the huge wolf-dog was staring right at him. He scrambled back from the edge but not before seeing the vicious animal run toward him.

Without hesitating, he jumped to his feet and raced away from the canyon where the white man lived.

As he fled, Dog's long legs took him quickly to the wind-gnarled pines where the Indian had lain, spying on those below. From that spot, the scent trail of the Indian was as plain as a broad highway to the nose of the beast, and he let loose a howl of victory as he turned to race after the Indian.

* * * * *

At the ramada below, Preacher and Budge were enjoying second cups of coffee when they heard Dog's howl. Hearing that, Preacher was a bit puzzled, because dog usually hunted in silence. But he quickly put the matter out of his mind. He knew Dog could handle anything short of an enraged grizzly bear. And even in that case, the bear was going to have a tough time. He turned his mind back to his conversation with Budge.

* * * * *

Tall Elk raced deeper into the mountains, knowing the huge wolf-dog was closing in on him by the second. As he ran, he saw a rock shelf ahead that rose maybe twenty feet above the forest floor on which he ran. If he could get on top of that shelf, he would be safe from the dog. When he reached the base of the shelf, he leaped with all his might to catch a projection of stone with his hands. With his feet scrambling against the face of the stone, he pulled himself up to where he could get a foothold and reach upward for another grip.

Before he could get clear, Dog was at the base of the cliff face and with a powerful leap, snapped his mighty jaws together at the Indian's feet. He missed by less than an inch, his glistening fangs snapped shut with the Indian's left moccasin gripped in them.

Snarling horribly, Dog threw himself at the cliff face again and again, trying to get at the Indian. But Tall Elk scrambled to the top of the cliff and disappeared into the forest above.

As the Indian vanished above, Dog sat on his haunches and studied the cliff in front of him, seeking some way to get to the top. Soon he realized that if he couldn't' get over it, he'd go around it. Turning to his left, he raced along the base of the cliff, seeking some way up.

After clearing the top of the rock shelf, Tall Elk took a few steps into the surrounding trees. But then he stopped, turned back to the cliff, and peeked below to make sure he was free of the wolfdog. He looked just in time to see the dog turn left and race along the cliff face. He knew the cunning animal was seeking a way to the top. Without thinking too much, the big Indian swung his legs back over the cliff and began slowly working his way back down where he had just fled upward.

The dog was cunning, but so was the Indian. Tall Elk made his way back to the bottom of the cliff, picked up his moccasin, and headed toward the canyon where the hated white man lived.

* * * * *

When Tall Elk returned to his vantage point above Preacher's home, he sat among the trees again to think. He now had a dual problem: how to get at the man he hated and how to stay away from the vicious wolfdog. He realized the dog was following his own man-scent. So, he had to do something about that first of all.

He walked half a mile away from the homesite before he found a place where he could climb down to where the creek ran over its sandy bed. He stepped into the creek and waded out to where the water was deepest. Then he began to scrub his body and clothing with handfuls of the white sand from the creek bed.

Tall Elk scrubbed himself until his skin bled in places before he was satisfied that his man-scent was gone. He climbed out of the creek and cut down a large bush of sage and began rubbing the pungent herb all over himself, trying to camouflage whatever scent remained.

When he was convinced that Dog could no longer pick up his scent, the big Indian returned to where he could spy on the home of the white man. This time he crawled further down the cliff to where he could look over the top of the stable and see into the yard.

Below, he could see the two men, the one he hated and the one with the strange legs, seated at the table under the ramada eating a late breakfast. The smell of the food lifting up to him set his mouth to watering. Now his thoughts turned to how he could get some of that food for himself. As he schemed for a way to get the food, he heard a deep angry growl behind him. Silly Indian! He could have stripped his skin right off his body, and Dog could still have picked up his scent.

* * * * *

When Tall Elk rolled over onto his back, he saw the ferocious visage of that huge Wolfhound standing over him. Dog's face was a terrifying depiction of hate and rage. His lips were peeled back in a snarl that exposed his massive, two-inch canine teeth dripping with saliva.

The big Indian brought his knees up to protect his chest and made a tiny, girlish sound in this throat. Dog growled again, and Tall Elk pushed backward with all the strength of his long legs. Unfortunately, that move shoved his massive chest and shoulders over the edge of the cliff where he lay. Gravity took over, and he executed a slow, lazy somersault before landing flat on his back on the hard ground twenty-five feet below. His head slammed into the ground with the sound of a smashing pumpkin.

Dog didn't hesitate. He let his huge body slide down the slight angle of the cliff face until he stood over the body of the hated enemy. Snarling, slavering, he eyed the Indian for any sign of life. A small pool of blood was forming behind the Indian's head. Dog pawed at Tall Elk's face, his thick claws cutting furrows in his cheeks. No response. He repeated that move several times with no reaction from the Indian.

Satisfied that Tall Elk no longer posed a threat to the man he loved, Dog stepped off the body, lifted his hind leg, and emptied his bladder on the Indian. Then he scratched mightily with his back legs, throwing dirt, leaves, and bits of straw over the prostrate form of his enemy. Now, highly pleased with himself, he trotted around the stable walls and hurried to where his master sat at the table under the ramada. Dog then curled up at his master's feet under the table and fell into a much-deserved sleep.

CHAPTER EIGHTEEN

Meanwhile, back in Contention, the once-lovely woman known as The Boss had become a caricature of herself. Her face and hands were pink with puckered scar tissue. Parts of her scalp had the same appearance where her long, auburn hair had been burned off, never to regrow.

And at the moment, her disposition was as hideous as her appearance. She stormed around the main room of the Silver Dollar Saloon, smacking with her cane at tables, chairs, even slow-moving outlaws who didn't get out of her way in time. Her current rage was directed at William Wells, her husband. After all her labor and expense in stealing her only child, James Wells, away from William, the cowardly thief had somehow managed to steal him back. She had just received confirmation that young James was now safely back in New Orleans with his father.

So many of the men who had once jumped to obey her every command now seemed to have disappeared. Who could she send to steal James back again? Who could she trust enough to know they would faithfully obey her orders that James must not be injured, but William *must* be killed to assure this problem never occurs again?

Her rage took her back to the long, polished bar and to where Hector, one of the bartenders, stood watching her. She raised the cane over her head, about to bring it down on his head.

But Hector simply caught the cane as she brought it down, wrenched it out of her hand and said, "There'll be none of that, Boss. We'll find somebody to send."

"Who? Who, blast you anyway! Who can I send? Where the heck is everyone, anyway? Where did all my men go?"

"Now, just take it easy, Boss. Some of the men..."

"Oh, shut up, you fool! Just find me someone. And make it fast!"

* * * * *

Who Hector was able to find was the man named Chancey. The man who had lost a shootout to the man who called himself Bill Rooney. The wounds

Chancey had received to both elbows were healing, but he would never again have the range of movement in his arms that he'd once had.

When Hector questioned him about making the trip to New Orleans to kill The Boss's husband and bring back her son, he jumped at the chance.

Not that he had any intention of dealing with either William or James Wells, but he would use The Boss's traveling funds to get himself back to New York City. There, in his one-time home, he would forget that he ever thought of himself as a gunman.

As Chancey left for Tombstone and the train station there, The Boss was able to calm her tortured soul for a while, confident that her orders would be obeyed.

* * * * *

Back in a small box canyon at the base of the Santa Catalina Mountains, a rare event was occurring. A steady, almost gentle rain was falling. Rain was infrequent in the desert, but generally when it came, it came hard. Violent. Howling, vicious wind and killing lightning. This was different. This was an easy rain. In that box canyon, all the buildings were dark. The only sound was the hissing of the rain on the roofs.

That silence was suddenly broken by a coughing, spluttering, choking sound as a sleeper awoke. He woke to find rain pouring into his nostrils, his mouth, his ears. The sleeper struggled to sit up. His arms at first refused to obey him. By sheer force of will, he made them lift his upper body. Pain like he'd never experienced shot through his head. He didn't know his skull had been fractured in his fall. He didn't even remember the fall. He forced his legs to bend, got his knees under him, and stood. He wavered, teetered, almost fell.

He took a step. Another. Came to a wall of stone. Blocks of stone. He felt along the stone wall, made his feet follow his hands. He came to the end of the wall. Everything was dark, but slightly less dark ahead. He made his stumbling feet go in that direction. He passed a corral, a ramada, a house. He wasn't aware of them.

His stumbling steps took him downhill. He stepped into running water. A small branch of Sabino Creek, normally only knee-deep, was running chest-deep with the rain runoff. He took one more step. His feet shot out from under him, and the rushing water carried him down stream. Tumbling, rolling, he was swept into the darkness.

75

CHAPTER NINETEEN

As Preacher stepped out of his cabin the next morning, he was greeted by the creosote smell of the freshly washed desert.

"Morning, Budge," he offered as he accepted a steaming cup of fresh coffee from his friend.

"Morning, Preacher." Budge responded. "That was sure enough a good rain we got last night. Needed it, I reckon."

"Yeah, I guess so. But luckily, it came at night. Much as I enjoy being clean, I flat out hate getting rained on!"

"I believe you've mentioned that a time or two...or three. Biscuits about ready to come out of the oven. What do you have planned for the day?"

"I have to go into town, pick up the mail. The check for that job in Contention should be there. Anything you need from there? Or do you want to come along?"

"Well, there's some supplies I should pick up, if you're sure you won't mind a little company."

"Wouldn't mind a bit! I'll hitch up the buggy right after we eat."

* * * * *

Several miles away, and only a hundred yards from the tiny village of Tanque Verde, a bronzed body lay where it had been deposited by falling flood waters. For a long time, the body didn't move. It might have been dead. A huge raven landed near the body, hopped close, and tilted its head to study the still form. Satisfied, the big bird took one more hop and pecked at the thin drizzle of blood that ran from the back of the body's head.

The quick jab of that sharp beak caused the body to jerk, and the startled bird jumped back, unfurled its huge wings, and flew to the top of a nearby dead cottonwood tree. From there it eyed the still form once more.

Slowly, the body stirred, began to move. Rolled over onto its back. Tall Elk opened his eyes to look around. He didn't know where he was. He didn't know *who* he was. All he knew was the pain inside his head was excruciating. It caused his empty belly to twist.

He forced himself to his feet. The movement made the pain in his head double. He was nearly forced to his knees, but before he fell, he spotted a thin plume of smoke rising in the still air. He grabbed at the bare branch of the dead tree and pulled himself out of the streambed where he had awakened. He had lost his shirt. He had lost his moccasins. He still had his breechclout. He still had his knife. He began making his way toward the smoke.

* * * * *

The tiny village of Tanque Verde consisted of five buildings. Four of them were built of adobe. One of them was abandoned; its roof starting to cave in. One of them was a Navajo hogan, built of mesquite logs. It was occupied by an ancient old man. He was alone, toothless, and just waiting to walk the sky road to the next world.

The largest of the adobes was a cantina. From the door of the cantina came the smell of frying bacon. That is where Tall Elk headed. A ramada of saguaro ribs shaded the door. He stepped up onto the boardwalk, stumbled, grabbed the wall to keep from falling, and stepped inside.

Two men were in the dim interior. One was standing behind a plain wood bar, polishing a glass. The other was seated at a table with a plate of bacon and beans in front of him.

Tall Elk walked unsteadily to that man and grabbed at the plate of food in front of him. The man immediately leaped to his feet and swung his fist into the face of the Indian who had just tried to steal his breakfast. Tall Elk was knocked off his feet, but he came back up far faster than the man would have believed possible. And he came up with that wickedly sharp Bowie knife in his hand.

A slashing swing of that knife caught the man right under the jaw and nearly cut his head off. The man fell to the floor, and Tall Elk again grabbed the plate of food and began stuffing it into his mouth with the hand not holding the knife.

The man behind the bar climbed over it with a stout club in his hand. "You filthy vermin! You lousy Injun! You...I'm gonna kill you!"

He raised the club over his head, but Tall Elk shoved that Bowie knife forward, the sharp blade sliding easily under the man's ribs and slicing his heart neatly in half. The second man was dead before he hit the ground.

Now Tall Elk laid his knife on the table and used both hands to push the food into his mouth. When the plate was empty, he saw the cup of coffee setting on the table and drained it in one swallow. He could not comprehend that there would be more food and more coffee in the tiny kitchen at the rear of the building. He didn't know what a kitchen was.

What he had eaten had strengthened him somewhat. His steps were a bit more certain. He put his knife back in its sheath and, stepping over the bodies of the two men he had just killed, went back outside.

* * * * *

Outside, on the splintered boardwalk, Tall Elk looked around. The only person in sight was the ancient Navajo sitting in the doorway of his hogan, watching the sun come up. He looked down, saw the Bowie knife, and moved toward the old Indian. As he stepped off the boardwalk, he stumbled, went to his knees. When he had struggled back to his feet, the old Indian was gone.

When Tall Elk looked behind him, the rising sun shining in his face hurt his eyes, so he turned to put the sun at his back and began to make his stumbling way down the road, following his shadow.

* * * * *

While Preacher went into the Arizona National Bank in Tucson to deposit his check, Budge headed for Miller's Mercantile Emporium to pick up his supplies. He was always amazed and a little awed by the vast array and variety of goods available there, all just for the asking. He still remembered with shame his days as Tucson's "town drunk," before Preacher befriended him, cleaned him up, and made a respectable man of him. Budge would forever be grateful to Preacher for what he had done for him. And he was always looking for ways to express his gratitude.

So, he was pleased to see Miller had a supply of crispy, red apples. Budge picked up half a dozen of them, intending to make an apple pie for their dinner tonight. That was one of Preacher's favorites.

* * * * *

Tall Elk continued to plod along the dirt track as the sun rose behind him and his shadow grew shorter before him. He slowly became aware that something large and black was just ahead of him. He failed to realize that it was a threat. He was coming up on a three-hundred-pound black bear that had been wounded by a careless hunter, two days before the rainstorm. The bear's left shoulder was shattered, making it difficult to move around and find food. But he had just recently come upon the carcass of a sheep that had been drowned in the storm.

The bear was near starved and not about to give up its meal. It rose up on its hind legs and roared a challenge, waving its good right paw to warn the Indian away. His huge claws glistened, wet with blood.

But in the depths of Tall Elk's injured brain, he took the gesture as a threat instead of a warning. He once again pulled out his vicious knife and strode purposefully toward the bear.

Seeing the Indian coming closer, the bear dropped down and ran, three-legged, straight at the Indian, snarling horribly. It was a false charge and stopped several feet short of Tall Elk. It was in the bear's nature to fake a charge like that to frighten off an enemy or a competitor.

The bear stopped short, but the Indian didn't. He kept coming right at the beast, so the bear again rose up on its hind legs and roared another challenge. He just wanted to eat his meal in peace.

When only a couple feet separated them, the Indian ran right at the big bear and buried his knife in the bear's already injured shoulder. The bear swung its right paw, with claws as big as a man's fingers, right at this enemy that had attacked and hurt him. That blow could have broken the neck of a large bull, but it caught the Indian on his left shoulder, breaking the collar bone and sending the Indian rolling off the road.

Tall Elk got hurriedly to his feet and ran back at the bear again, this time holding his knife low and blade up. The bear grabbed the Indian in what would have been a death grip had he not already lost the use of his left paw. But he held the Indian close and sank his huge teeth into the Indian's already injured left shoulder, bones snapping under those massive jaws. But the Indian sank his knife blade into the bear's belly and pulled the blade up, disemboweling the creature.

The bear made a coughing 'woof', like a domestic dog, released its grip on the Indian, rolled over on its side, and died.

Tall Elk stood over the vanquished enemy, his shattered left arm hanging at his side, and wondered what he should do now. Nothing registered in the fog of his brain, so he wiped his knife blade on the bear's fur and stepped back on the road and continued his shambling walk.

CHAPTER TWENTY

Preacher finished loading up Budge's purchases from the Mercantile and climbed up to the buggy seat. As he picked up the reins, Budge asked, "Would you mind swinging by the Cooper's place on the way home? I heard at the store that they were butchering some hogs, and I'd like to pick up a couple hams to smoke."

"Sure, that's alright with me. Some ham sounds mighty good." Preacher swung the buggy around and headed south out of town instead of north. The Cooper place wasn't all that far out of the way. And they did raise some mighty nice hogs. As they rode, the sun swung past midday and started its slow slide down the western sky.

* * * * *

Tall Elk continued his stumbling, staggering walk west. He had stuck his left hand inside the cord that tied his breechclout. That arm hanging loose was causing him too much pain as it flopped around. It was better when the arm didn't move. As he walked, heat waves shimmered in the distance.

Coming out of those heat waves, a couple miles ahead, came two small wagons. Identical wagons, side by side. He raised his right hand to shade his eyes and when that hand covered his right eye, the two wagons magically transformed into one. He'd been seeing double for quite a while, but this was the first time the two had become one. He decided it must be magic. Spirits playing tricks on him. He moved his hand away and the wagon became two wagons again. Two wagons, two horses, four men.

He moved his hand back in front of his face, and the two wagons became one again. One wagon, one horse, two men. This was interesting. Fun, almost. Every time he closed one eye, there was one. Open that eye and there were two. What were the spirits trying to tell him? He kept walking slowly, barely moving. And he kept opening and closing one eye, making a wagon appear and disappear.

* * * * *

Budge touched Preacher's shoulder. "Looky there! A couple miles ahead. There's somebody walking. Looks like he's hurt."

Budge's eyesight had always been sharp. He was picking up something Preacher could barely make out. Preacher could vaguely see a shape among the heat shimmers but couldn't tell if it was a person or a tree stump.

He shook the reins for Budge's mare to pick up the pace a bit, but it was way too hot to make the horse work any harder than it had to. Whatever it was ahead of them, they'd get to it sooner or later.

* * * * *

Tall Elk had long since ceased to think logically. His many injuries and his deprivation had robbed him of reason. He was now operating solely on the primitive, lizard part of his brain. He was reacting with pure animal cunning. The road he was on dropped down to cross a rain-carved gully, and the wagon he had been watching momentarily disappeared. As soon as he was out of sight, he stepped off the road and hid himself behind a large fallen saguaro.

* * * * *

Budge had been watching the approaching figure with curiosity tinged with a touch of alarm. He didn't know why the figure should concern him, but he had long since learned to listen to those leadings. So, he noticed when the figure dropped into a dip in the road, and he was also aware that the figure didn't come *out* of that dip.

When the wagon reached the point where the figure had vanished, Budge saw staggering impressions in the thick dust of the road that simply vanished. He looked all around and saw nothing.

"Huh! That's odd," he said.

Preacher answered, "What's odd?"

"Well, that injured guy we saw on the road. He's gone. From the tracks, it looks like he just flew away."

"Now, Pard, you know that's not possible. What *is* possible is that those eagle eyes of yours just played a trick on you, and there wasn't really anybody there to begin with."

"Well…I suppose that's it." Budge replied. "But it sure 'nough looked like somebody hurt."

"Either way, I don't imagine it matters much. Let's get those hams back home."

As the wagon rolled past, Tall Elk eased his long body up from where he had hidden, made his way back to the road, and turned to follow the tracks of the wagon. The thirst for revenge now drove him. Revenge for what, he no longer could recall. He just allowed the emotion to lead him. The wagon was soon out of sight. He followed the tracks in the dust.

* * * * *

When the two friends finally arrived back at the stone cabin in that box canyon, Dog ran out of the stable to greet them. Preacher rubbed his ears for a bit and then helped Budge hang the two large hams in the smoke house. Budge laid a fire in the stove and added several pieces of green mesquite. Soon fragrant smoke was pouring from the chimney.

Dog stood for a long time, staring down the road before returning to the ramada where Budge and Preacher were preparing their supper. Before long, shadows claimed the canyon, stars appeared, and night reigned. Far down the road, a stumbling figure doggedly followed the wagon tracks.

* * * * *

Back in Contention, the scarred, twisted figure of what had once been a beautiful woman known as The Boss, stood dejectedly at the bar of the Silver Dollar Saloon. She wore a lovely green dress that had once fit her so perfectly, flattering her woman's figure, but which now hung from her body like scraps caught in a tree.

The only image that moved in the large mirror behind the bar was her own. All the people who once jumped at her every word were gone. They had all deserted her, and she was alone. In disgust, she picked up the coal oil lamp from the bar beside her and heaved it with all her might at the freak show image staring back at her from that mirror.

Because of the scars on her arms, that throw came up short and fell among the rows of bottles behind the bar. Bottles of tequila, mescal, rye whiskey, all that alcohol erupted in a fireball that blew outward and engulfed the woman once feared and revered as The Boss. As she fell screaming into the inferno, the hungry flames licked at the walls of the saloon, spread to the building next door. The night wind made sure that, before that fire burned itself out, little would be left of what was once called Contention.

* * * * *

The stars wheeled overhead of the peaceful box canyon in the foothills of the Santa Catalina Mountains of Southern Arizona Territory. The moon rose and set on the comfortable homesite. Nothing moved.

And then something did. Out on the road, a dim figure slowly appeared. A shambling, staggering figure of what had once been a strong and proud warrior of the Apache people. Tall Elk was now little more than a caricature of what he had been. Hunger, thirst, horrible injuries, had left him nothing more than a puppet fueled by rage, hate, and the need for revenge. He continued to stumble along in the wake of the tracks he had followed for so long.

He came to the place where the tracks stopped, turned from the road and into that peaceful homesite. Tall Elk stopped there, also, swaying back and forth on his feet. The enemy he had trailed for so long was here. The man he must kill was here. He fumbled with his right hand for the knife that hung from his left hip. Finally, he was able to pull it free. Holding the blade before him, he stepped from the road and into the neat yard in front of him.

As soon as Tall Elk's feet hit the dirt yard of Preacher's home, Dog awoke with a start. Instantly, he was alert. He rose to his feet from his bed in the straw where he slept next to Jim's stall. A low rumbling growl began deep in his throat. Stiff-legged, every sense keenly alert, Dog moved around the corner of the house to the yard where he knew his enemy, the enemy of the man he loved, had come seeking revenge.

Silent as a wraith, Dog stalked toward where the big Indian stood by the road. When Tall Elk saw the hellhound stalking slowly toward him, something inside him turned to water and the temptation to turn and run was strong. But no! His hate overcame his fear. He faced the huge dog and, with his wicked knife held out before him, began walking to meet the threat.

At four feet away, Dog stopped. His yellow eyes burned into the fever-bright eyes of the Indian. He saw fear there. And he saw hatred. Dog knew this fight would be to the death. He also knew it would be a short fight. He gathered his hind legs under him, prepared to leap at the throat of this enemy.

The enemy saw the movement and knew what the hellhound would do. So, when Dog began his leap at Tall Elk's throat, the Indian swung his razor-sharp blade, seeking to bury it in the dog's heart.

But as soon as Dog began his leap, he stopped, dropped down and then backed up. The Indian's knife sailed harmlessly past, and Dog sank his wicked canines into Tall Elk's right forearm. Those massive jaws clamped shut on that arm: bones were crushed and arteries were ruptured. Tall Elk screamed, and Dog began shaking his massive head back and forth like a terrier worrying at a rat. The scream brought Preacher from his house, pistol in hand.

By the waning light of the moon, he saw the scene before him and recognized the Indian who had once challenged him to combat. How and why that Indian was now at his own home and being brutalized by Dog, he had no idea.

Tall Elk took his eyes off the dog that was trying to break his arm when he saw the hated man standing over him. With a super-human effort, the big Indian ignored the beast that had his right arm and wrenched his damaged left hand from the cord of his breechclout and grabbed for the knife that had fallen from his hand.

But as soon as his hand touched the blade, Dog dropped that arm and dove at the Indian's throat. One quick slashing bite took out arteries, muscles, and windpipe. With an audible sigh, Tall Elk fell back and died.

Dog quickly positioned himself between the Indian and his master and watched the fallen foe for any sign of continued threat. Preacher laid his hand on Dog's head as Budge came hurrying around the corner with a shotgun in his hands.

He saw the scene before him. The dead Indian, the protective Dog, and Preacher standing there as puzzled as he himself was. "What the heck was this all about?" he wondered.

Preacher said, "I don't know what to tell you. I just got here myself. But it looks like Dog has everything under control."

He knelt down beside the huge dog and rubbed his head. "Sure do wish sometimes that you could talk, old pal," he said. "I sure would like to know what this was all about. But, c'mon inside, pal. Let's get some light and make sure you aren't hurt. I'll clean up this mess come morning."

Soon darkness returned to the box canyon. Peaceful quiet came back, too.

CHAPTER TWENTY-ONE

Preacher buried the body of Tall Elk across the creek that flowed past his stone cabin. The Indian's Bowie knife, he kept. Hung it from a wall inside the cabin as a memory of the mystery of what the Indian had been doing there in the first place. The mystery that only Dog knew the answer to, and he wasn't talking.

The smell of the hams curing in the smokehouse warred with the aroma of hot apple pie baking in the oven by the ramada. Preacher lingered over a third cup of Budge's delicious coffee.

The two friends sat talking quietly at the table. Budge asked, "Well, what kinda plans do you have? Any new jobs coming up?"

"Nope. That job in Contention paid enough that I won't have to work again for the rest of the year. Unless something interesting comes up, that is. I believe, come Fall, I might take a ride up Wyoming way. There's a ranch up there I'd like to take a look at."

"Wyoming, huh? I've never been up there. Hear it's a right pretty place, though."

"Well shoot, why don't we just hitch up the buggy and both go then?"

"Really? You wouldn't mind if I went along?"

"'Course not, Budge. That's what friends are for. Shoot, we could even take the train, if you'd be more comfortable."

"By golly, you got a deal! I'll be looking forward to that, yes, sir!"

Sitting high atop a tall saguaro, a mockingbird added his song to the peaceful scene below.

THE END